Something crashed into Slocum's skull, sending him spinning to the floor. He clawed for his gun, his vision clouded by winking lights from the blow to his head. Whirling over on his side, he aimed his Peacemaker toward a shadowy shape towering over him and quickly tightened his finger on the trigger.

A boot struck his gun hand, knocking the Colt from his grasp before he could get off a shot. His gun went clattering into a corner of the room, but not before Slocum crawfished backward as fast as he could, reaching into his shirt for the .32 bellygun. In a flash he had his smaller gun cocked and ready to fire, and the sound of a cocking pistol stopped the figure looming over him from coming any closer.

"I'll kill you!" Slocum swore, his head still reeling from being struck. "One step closer and I'll make a hole through your belly . . ."

JAKE LOGAN

SLOCUM AND THE LADY FROM ABILENE

JOVE BOOKS, NEW YORK

SLOCUM AND THE LADY FROM ABILENE

A Jove Book / published by arrangement with
the author

PRINTING HISTORY
Jove edition / August 1999

The Penguin Putnam Inc. World Wide Web site address is
http://www.penguinputnam.com

ISBN: 0-515-12555-5

A JOVE BOOK®
Jove Books are published by The Berkley Publishing Group,
a division of Penguin Putnam Inc.,
375 Hudson Street, New York, New York 10014.
JOVE and the "J" design
are trademarks belonging to Penguin Putnam Inc.

PRINTED IN THE UNITED STATES OF AMERICA

10 9 8 7 6 5 4 3 2 1

SLOCUM AND THE
LADY FROM ABILENE

1

John Slocum liked the feel of open country almost as much as he savored the charms of a beautiful woman—depending on how long he'd been denied one or the other, he decided. Riding across a grassy prairie toward the Texas town of Abilene, he told himself he'd seen enough of rolling hills and scrub live-oak trees for a spell. What he needed now was a woman. And Abilene had plenty of them in its variety of saloons clustered near the railroad depot. The town also had more than its share of men with bad dispositions. It was developing a reputation as a robbers' roost where the law didn't interfere all that much, just so long as the tough hombres in the saloon district killed or robbed only each other. But when an honest citizen happened to step in front of a knife or a bullet, the Texas Rangers were called in. And if there was one bunch of lawmen nobody wanted to tangle with, it was the Rangers.

While it was true most Rangers were sincere enforcers of the law, on occasion the governor of Texas saw nothing wrong with fighting fire with fire. A handful of Rangers Slocum had met over the years were only a notch or two above being hired killers, paid assassins working for the state to rid its borders of unsavory types by any means at hand . . . usually meaning a gun, or a rope tied to a tree limb without benefit of a trial, a judge, or a jury. Some said it was justified, saving the taxpayers the expense of a long trial, or the chance that sympathetic jurors might set a guilty man free. In the eyes of many citizens, old-fashioned Ranger justice worked just fine, and in most cases there were few complaints when a murderer or a horse thief met his untimely end in some remote part of Texas, swinging at the end of a rope or with a bullet hole in his head. A Fort Worth newspaper gave one such account a front-page story, with the Ranger's official report listing the cause of death as "accidental strangulation" in the case of an escaped murderer named Red Lopez. Lopez had apparently placed a hangman's noose around his own neck and then accidentally fallen off his horse with his hands tied behind him.

Riding west over a string of low hills, Slocum caught sight of Abilene, the outlines of a few two-story buildings near the center of town and dozens of dusty streets crisscrossing a town built along a railroad line. Most of the structures were made of weathered clapboard. Stores with false fronts lined busier roads through the business district. Whitewashed homes with long front and rear porches denoted the residential areas of Abilene's better-heeled citizens, while clusters of smaller shacks were bunched together in poorer sections of town.

In summer, Abilene could be one of the hottest places on earth, with temperatures well above a hundred for days on end. Taylor County, with Abilene as its county seat, was one of the driest parts of middle Texas most of the year. As Slocum rode closer, a pall of chalky dust rose into the air from wagon and buggy wheels, and the hooves of horses moving up and down the city's streets. Just the sight of so much dust gave Slocum a powerful thirst . . . but not for water or lemonade or anything of the kind. Good whiskey was what he sought, if it could be had this far west. Kentucky whiskey, especially his favorite, the sour-mash variety, was hard to find in dusty cattle towns, and it came at a substantial price when he found it.

His big Palouse stud struck a faster trot, sensing the nearness of a stable, a bucket of oats, and a rack of hay, with straw bedding for comfort after better than a hundred miles of hard riding coming up from the Mexican border. Slocum had sold two blooded Thoroughbred stallions at Hidalgo to a wealthy Mexican rancher, a horse breeder who wanted to improve his herd. Thus it was that Slocum was headed back to Denver with Mexican gold in his money belt, a hefty sum from the sale of prize racing stock. Some men would have worried over carrying so much money across hundreds of miles to Denver; however, Slocum wasn't the worrying kind when it came to handling men with dishonest intentions. He knew how to take care of himself and he carried all the tools he needed: a Colt .44/.40 revolver, a .32-caliber bellygun tucked inside his shirt, a Winchester .44 repeating rifle, and perhaps the deadliest of all his weapons, a Greener ten-gauge sawed-off shotgun that would tear a man to shreds at twenty paces or less. Good aim wasn't all that important with the Greener. Firing in someone's general direction was usually all that was needed to bring him down, and in most cases when some owlhoot went down in front of the Greener, he stayed down.

Dusk came creeping across the hills as Slocum headed toward the outskirts of town.

The largest saloon in Abilene was named the Silver Spur, and Slocum had visited it before. It catered to a better clientele, and kept most saddle tramps and troublemakers out by means of an armed doorman who insisted that guns be checked with him before going inside. When Slocum came through the bat-wing doors, a burly fellow with a thick black beard and a brace of pistols held up a beefy palm to halt him at the entrance.

"Gotta check that gun, mister," he said. "House rules."

Slocum unbuckled his cross-pull holster and handed it over to the doorman.

"That's a shootist's rig," the doorman said. "Don't see many cross-draws, 'cept in the hands of hired gunmen, and there ain't all that many of that troublesome breed who use a cross-draw. You're either a mighty good shot, or a feller lookin' to get hisself killed."

Slocum grinned politely. "I'm sure as hell not lookin' to get killed, and I don't reckon my aim is nowhere near perfect. I came after a bottle of Kentucky sour mash, if such a thing can be had in this town."

"We've got the finest. Just ask that gent behind the bar for your favorite brand."

Slocum nodded, and had turned for the bar across an all-but-empty drinking parlor when the doorman's voice halted him.

"If you are a hired shooter, stranger, don't cause no trouble in this establishment. Just a little friendly advice."

It was almost enough to get Slocum's dander up, but his overpowering thirst for good whiskey kept him from saying more than he should. "Like I said, all I want is some Kentucky whiskey and a quiet place to drink it." He turned back again, and sauntered across a polished wood floor to a long mahogany bar with mirrors behind it. A balding man with green garters on his shirtsleeves came over.

"What'll it be, mister?"

"Kentucky sour mash, the best you've got."

"We've got Gold Label, the best there is. Costs four bits a glass, poured plumb to the rim."

"Start pourin'," Slocum replied, taking a handful of bank notes from his pants pocket. "I'll tell you when to stop, and when I get ready to leave you can price me the rest of the bottle.''

The bartender only needed a glimpse of Slocum's money before he reached under the bar, taking out a fresh jug of Gold Label Kentucky Special. He uncorked it and sniffed the cork, smiling as he reached behind him for a clean shot glass. ''You can pour fer yourself, stranger,'' he added. ''I could tell when you come in you was a man of means, even with all that trail dust on yer coat an' hat. Whereabouts you headed?'' He put the glass down in front of Slocum, waiting for an answer.

''Up to Denver. Just passin' through. I was here before a few years ago. Nicest place in town.'' He poured himself a glass of whiskey and tasted it, making sure it wasn't watered and then colored with carmel or tobacco in order to fool lesser men. It was pure sour mash. He tossed the rest of the contents down his throat and began pouring again. ''It used to be some of the bars down the street were rough places to hang your hat. I reckon it's still the same, especially later at night.''

''Plenty of shootin' goes on. We got us a gutless marshal an' a pair of knock-kneed young deputies who stay the hell away from most of them places. The City Council keeps tryin' to hire a real lawman who ain't afraid of them tough types, only the job don't pay enough to draw nobody who's any good at keepin' the peace. That's how come we keep Clyde over yonder at the door, checkin' guns. He can be meaner'n hell if he needs to be, an' he's a real good shot when he's up close. His eyes ain't none too good at a distance, but he keeps things quiet inside the Silver Spur. Just ask anybody in town. Won't hardly nobody tangle with Clyde.''

Slocum knew one more thing about Clyde, and his eyes. They hadn't been good enough to spot the .32 hidden under his shirt and coat. ''That's a comfort,'' Slocum told the barman. "Makes a man feel safer havin' a drink here, knowing nobody gets inside with a gun." He tossed back his second drink and poured a third with an eye on a box of rum-soaked cheroots behind the bar. "I think I'll have one of those good cigars too. On second thought, hand me half a dozen. Give me the rum-flavored variety. Sure does make sweet smoke."

The barkeep removed six cigars from the box. "You sure do have a taste fer expensive things, mister. These cigars is ten cents apiece."

Slocum took one and bit off the twisted end, reaching for a Lucifer in his coat pocket. "If a man's gonna drink he may as well drink the best there is. Same goes for smo-kin' and plenty of other things. I ride the best horses money can buy. Worst predicament on earth is bein' stranded in the middle of nowhere with a crippled mount, or one that doesn't have any stamina or speed. A good saddle keeps a man's butt from being sore on long rides. A gun that isn't well made can get a man killed if he has a misfire."

The bartender nodded. "Not just everybody can afford the best. Seems you can, without a doubt. Mind if I ask what sort of business you're in?"

"I'm in the horse business. Blooded race stock. Every now and then I take on a few other lines of work. Not nearly so often lately."

The barman seemed satisfied as he took a few bills from Slocum's stack of currency, counting out silver change for the whiskey and cigars. "You're obviously a successful man, Mr . . . ?"

"Slocum. John Slocum."

"They call me Gus. Pleased to meet you, Mr. Slocum, an' you're always welcome here at the Silver Spur."

"I need a good room for the night, Gus. What would you recommend in the way of a hotel?"

"Ain't but one that'll suit you. The Cattleman's Inn over

on Baker Street. Good beds. Good food downstairs in the dinin' room, maybe the best in Abilene. Mostly rich cattle buyers from up north stay there, or big ranchers come to town to sell their herds.''

"I'm obliged for the information. I'll hire a stable for my stud and see about a room at the Cattleman's.''

Gus frowned when he looked out a front window. "I see you came ridin' that spotted animal at the hitch rail. Most horsemen in these parts ain't got much use fer a two-color horse.''

Slocum shrugged. "Then most horsemen around here don't know a damn thing about good horses. A Palouse can outlast damn near any breed on the trail, and they're tougher'n boot leather. They come from up north in Idaho Territory.''

Gus still appeared skeptical. "All the same, a feller would have a hard time convincin' most folks there's such a thing as a good two-color horse. Ain't that I'm doubtin' your word on it, but it's hard to change some folks' minds on certain things when they get a particular notion.''

A commotion down the street drew their attention, angry men shouting at each other.

Clyde took a double-barrel shotgun from a rack behind him and went to the swinging doors.

Slocum turned, leaning on one elbow, smoking his cheroot with his whiskey glass in his left hand. "Wonder what that's all about,'' he said to Gus.

"Prob'ly trouble at the Wagon Wheel,'' he said. "Lately we've had more'n our share of gunslicks in town, hangin' around at the Wagon Wheel. Feller by the name of Davis . . . Justin Davis he calls hisself. Him an' his bunch have shot up that end of town a few times. There's four who ride with Davis. Don't none of 'em look like tinhorns.''

A shot rang out, echoing up and down the street, the crack of a pistol.

Clyde tightened his grip on his shotgun. "They'd better not bring their damn fight down here," he muttered. "Can't see real good who it was got shot. Some poor bastard is layin' in the middle of the road, holdin' onto his belly."

2

With the bottle of Gold Label in his fist and the cigars in his coat pocket, Slocum ambled out the doors of the Silver Spur just as a crowd gathered around the wounded man farther down the road. He could hear someone moaning. Cowboys and storekeepers stood in a circle where the downed man lay. While Slocum put his whiskey in his saddlebags, he heard someone yell, "Go fetch Doc Greenwood an' Marshal Hatcher quick!" The street running beside the depot was dark, making it hard to see clearly especially as a large crowd had been drawn to the scene by the gunshot and by the cries of pain coming from whoever caught the bullet.

"Don't nobody go nowhere!" a rasping voice demanded. "Let the sumbitch die."

Slocum turned toward the voice, sighting a tall, raw-boned man with a pistol dangling at his side, a dusty flop-brim cowboy hat covering most of his face. It was Slocum's nature to avoid troubles that weren't his. He'd had more than his share over the years and didn't need to buy into any. But when a wounded man was being denied a doctor by some rough-talking bully with a gun, Slocum decided he couldn't just walk away. He could make out the silhou-

9

ette of the gunman in light spilling from a window of the
Wagon Wheel Saloon.

He buckled on his gunbelt and removed the hammer
thong on his Colt, pulling his coattail away from the butt
of the pistol as he walked toward the crowd. A young cowboy lay in a pool of blood, rocking back and forth, groaning, his face twisted in agony while he gripped a bullet
hole in his stomach that was pumping more blood onto the
caliche road.

Slocum edged nearer until he faced the gunman standing
over the wounded boy. This might be the gent Gus had said
was Justin Davis. Slocum knew the names of most truly
dangerous gunmen across the West, with few exceptions.
He'd never heard of Justin Davis.

"Go get a doctor," Slocum said to a man in a storekeeper's apron standing beside him. "Hurry. This kid ain't
gonna last long unless he gets some help."

Slocum knew what would come next. The gunman gave
him an icy stare.

"Didn't you hear what I just said, mister?" he snarled,
his fingers closing around the grips on the pistol dangling
next to his right leg. "I said let the little sumbitch die."

"I heard what you said," Slocum replied evenly, staring
into the face of the shooter, his own right thumb hooked
in his gunbelt within easy reach of his .44/.40. "Don't give
a damn what you want, you yellow son of a bitch. This
feller next to me is going for the sawbones, and if you try
to stop him I'll blow you outta your goddamn boots. I'll
be givin' you every advantage. You've already got your
gun out. Just swing it up and aim it at me whenever you
take the notion. But you won't have time to get off a shot.
You've got my word on that. Try me . . . if you've got the
backbone, which I figure you ain't. You shot a boy who
ain't hardly old enough to shave, and in my book that

makes you a sack of yellow dog shit. Make your play, big man. I'm ready whenever you are.''

The storekeeper alongside Slocum backed away, then wheeled and took off running up the street. Everyone standing around the scene of the shooting was staring silently at Slocum, then back at the other man. The only sound was the wounded boy's soft cries.

''You've got a big mouth, stranger,'' the gunman snarled. ''A real big mouth.''

Slocum gave him a one-sided grin. ''And I can back it up, so raise that gun, or put it away.''

''I'm Justin Davis. Nobody talks to me like that!'' Still, Davis made no move to lift his pistol, staring hard into Slocum's eyes.

''I don't give a shit who you are,'' Slocum said. ''I already know two things about you, Davis. You're a coward who tries to make a name for himself shootin' down little boys. The other thing I'm real sure of is that you won't make a play for me. You'll turn around and walk off.''

Davis jutted his square jaw. ''An' why's that, you big-talkin' bastard? What makes you so sure I won't up an' kill you first?''

''Because you know I'll kill *you*. I can see it written all over your face. A coward's eyes get this hollow look when he's scared, like lookin' through the window of an empty house. You're afraid of dying, and you know damn well that's what's about to happen if you test your luck against me.''

Davis's anger was almost out of control. His muscles tensed after hearing another insult, although he kept his pistol at his side. ''Ain't no son of a bitch ever called me a coward an' lived to tell about it.''

''I'm still here, and I sure as hell am callin' you a yellow coward. Only, things just got a helluva lot worse for you. Now it ain't gonna be so easy, like before.''

"How's that?" Davis hissed, his teeth clamped together with everyone on the street watching him being challenged, his cheeks working furiously.

"You just called me a son of a bitch, and unless you apologize in front of all these good folks, I'm gonna have to kill you or whip your ass with my bare hands. Either way suits the hell outta me. Put the gun away and we'll settle this with fists, or jerk that iron up and let's start trading lead. The only other choice you've got is to start making that apology."

"To hell with you an' your . . ." Davis ended what he was about to say suddenly when Slocum started walking around the wounded man to the spot where Davis was standing.

Slocum stopped directly in front of Davis, only a yard of distance between them. "One last time," Slocum told him in a quiet voice. "Apologize, or I'm gonna start teaching you some manners. You won't like the way I teach school."

Davis had reached his boiling point, something Slocum had been counting on. Davis started to swing the muzzle of his gun toward Slocum's belly, giving Slocum plenty of warning when he tightened the muscles in his right shoulder only a fraction of a second beforehand.

Slocum's left fist flew out to grab Davis's wrist, and in the same instant he whipped out his Colt and stabbed it into Davis's belly. Davis froze, terror in his eyes the moment he realized his gun hand was caught in an iron grip and a pistol was aimed into his stomach.

"Bang!" Slocum said, grinning without a trace of humor. "You'd be dead now, from a bullet that busted your spine, only I decided to give you another chance to think it over, the business about an apology for callin' me a son of a bitch. How do you feel about it now?"

There were whispers in the crowd gathered around them,

remarks about how fast Slocum's pistol had come out, and how he'd been quick enough to grab Davis's wrist.

Davis swallowed. A slight tremor went down his arms and when he spoke, his tone was gentler. "I reckon I'm sorry I called you a son of a bitch, mister."

"Now drop the gun," Slocum demanded. "Then turn around and walk away. Go someplace else and stay there, because if I see your ugly face again tonight, I may change my mind and kill you just to see how long it takes you to die. Some gents can suffer for hours, if you shoot 'em in just the right place."

Davis's pistol thudded to the dirt. Slocum released his grip on the man's wrist and slowly lowered the hammer on his Colt. "I said turn around and clear out," Slocum reminded. "Don't make me say it again."

Davis took a step backwards, and when he did some of his courage returned. "I got friends," he said soft and low. "We may meet up again sometime."

"Bring your friends," Slocum told him. "Give 'em my personal invitation to come along. For your sake, I hope they've got more guts than you've got, 'cause they're gonna need 'em. Like I told you before, you turned out to be mighty short in the backbone department. You're yellow, Davis, trying to make a reputation shooting little boys. Next time you've got the urge to shoot at somebody, come lookin' for me. My name's John Slocum, and I'll be happy to oblige you damn near anytime. I'll stand real still and let you have the first pull."

Davis wheeled and stalked off, muttering to himself. Slocum picked up the gunman's pistol and turned his attention to the boy lying in the street behind him.

A bearded cowboy spoke to Slocum. "That was real brave, what you done, backin' down Justin Davis. But if'n I was you I'd keep one eye open at night. Davis ain't the kind to forget what you done to him in front of everybody."

"I'm not worried," Slocum said, kneeling, examining the hole in the kid's belly. "This boy's gutshot. Not much can be done for him, I'm afraid. Did anybody see the shooting?"

"I seen it," another man said, "only I'm keepin' my mouth shut 'bout what I saw. Davis would hunt me down an' kill me if I told the law what happened. I didn't see nothin'."

Slocum looked toward the speaker. "Then it wasn't a fair fight? This kid didn't draw first?"

"I done tol' you I didn't see nothin'. Forgit what I said before." He wheeled and hurried away from the spot with his hands shoved into his pants pockets.

A man in a derby hat carrying a medical bag came hurrying down the road.

"Yonder's Doc Greenwood," someone said.

Slocum stood up, sighing, knowing there was nothing anyone could do to stop the young cowboy's internal bleeding. Slocum had seen hundreds of wounds like this during the war, and almost no one recovered.

He spoke to the others standing around the cowboy just as the doctor arrived. "If any of you have a trace of backbone, you'd tell your marshal what happened here and Davis would be in jail facing a murder charge."

An old man with gray sideburns chuckled. "You must be real new in Abilene. Marshal Hatcher's scared of his own shadow, an' he sure as hell wouldn't think of tryin' to arrest Justin Davis on no murder charge. Bill Hatcher would go fishin' till this blowed over. We ain't got much in the way of a marshal here, in case you didn't know. Nobody wants the job. Last three lawmen the City Council hired quit, or got shot all to pieces. John Pickman died of the gangrene after he got shot. Only thing this town can do is send a wire fer the Rangers."

"Someone should notify the Texas Rangers about what happened here tonight," Slocum said.

"Not me," the old man replied. "I mind my own business an' duck down real low soon as I hear the first gunshot. I'll stay alive a lot longer this way."

Slocum shrugged, holstering his .44/.40. "It's your town. You folks are the ones who've gotta live here. Don't make a damn bit of difference to me."

He started back toward his horse, glancing over his shoulder every now and then to make certain Davis and some of his friends weren't coming after him. When he came to the watering trough in front of the Silver Spur, he tossed Davis's pistol into the water before loosening the stud's reins.

Clyde's voice from the entrance into the Silver Spur stopped him from mounting his horse. "I seen what you did, Mr. Slocum. I said when you came in earlier wearin' that cross-draw rig that you was either real good with a gun, or lookin' to git yourself killed. My eyes ain't all that good these days, but I seen you pull iron on Davis. Could be that was the fastest draw I ever seen in my life."

Slocum stuck a boot in the left stirrup and swung up on the Palouse. "Maybe like you said, your eyes ain't all that good. There's plenty who'll be faster'n me. Mr. Davis just didn't happen to be one of 'em."

Clyde chuckled. "Before you ride off, there's somebody else who saw what happened from an upstairs window. A lady, an' she said she'd like to meet you over a glass of brandy maybe, if you have the time."

Slocum glanced up at the second floor. An open window with a lantern aglow in the room behind it revealed the outline of a beautiful woman in a nightdress, open at the neck just enough to reveal plenty of cleavage. He took off his hat and bowed politely. "Evening, ma'am," he said.

"Good evening, sir," a lilting voice replied. "I asked

Clyde to invite you inside for a drink. Will you accept my invitation?''

"Gladly," he told her, stepping off his horse, and tying it up again. "Shall I meet you at a certain table inside?"

She smiled, and he could see rows of even white teeth, and perfect dimples in her milky cheeks despite poor light from a night sky overhead.

"If you prefer," she said, "Clyde can show you upstairs to my room. I saw how easily and bravely you handled Justin Davis, and I may have a business proposition for you."

Slocum grinned. "It just so happens I'm a businessman, so I'd naturally be inclined to listen to most any business proposition."

"Clyde will show you upstairs," she said. "However, you must still observe house rules and leave your gun with him."

"That won't be a problem, ma'am. I'll be right up, Miss . . . ?"

"Amanda. Amanda Drake."

"I'm John Slocum, and I'm pleased to make your acquaintance, Miss Drake."

He unbuckled his gun belt and followed Clyde through the swinging doors, thinking how good fortune had come his way. He had found the type of good whiskey he wanted, and now it seemed he'd found a beautiful woman. It was a hard combination to beat in Slocum's estimation.

"My horse," he said, handing Clyde his gun and holster. "I need to stable it and do something about my gear."

"I'll see to it, Mr. Slocum. I'll have our shine boy bring your gear up to Miss Drake's room after a bit."

Slocum turned for a stairway leading to the second floor.

"It's room number five," Clyde said. "It'll be on your left soon as you git to the top."

3

A statuesque brunette answered his knock. She smiled warmly and stepped back to admit him into an elegantly furnished lamplit bedroom; however, he paid scant notice to the expensive furnishings. Amanda Drake wore a silky white robe with lace around the neckline, its sash tied loosely around her slender waist so that the garment fell open at the top, showing the cleft between two milky mounds of flesh.

"Come in, Mr. Slocum," she purred, beckoning him toward an upholstered chair placed near the window, where a cool spring breeze lifted thin blue curtains away from the window frame until they settled back against the wall again.

A crystal decanter of sparkling amber brandy sat on a small table next to the offered chair. Two crystal goblets rested on the table, one with dark golden liquid filling it halfway to the rim. "Please take a seat and pour yourself a drink," she continued in a throaty voice.

He pulled off his hat, frowning briefly at the trail dust on the brim and crown, before passing fingers quickly through his unshorn, coal-black hair, in order to look as presentable as he could, under the circumstances, after three days of sleeping on hard ground between the border and

Abilene. "Thank you, ma'am," he said as she closed the door behind him. "A glass of brandy sounds mighty good right about now." He touched the dark beard stubble covering his chin. The last thing he needed now was to be forced into a situation where he had to make a good impression on a real lady. But when opportunity knocked, Slocum was never one to ignore it.

Amanda came over to take his hat. "Let me hang your coat and hat in the corner," she said. A coat tree stood in the corner next to a folding dressing screen.

"Sorry about the dust," he said, sleeving out of his split-tail frock coat, an expensive tailored piece of clothing he'd had made for him personally in Saint Louis. "I just rode into town. Haven't had time to hire a hotel room or find a decent bathhouse yet."

"I understand," Amanda replied, placing his hat on a peg and then hanging his coat beside it.

She walked over to the table with a seductive look on her face. "Don't worry about dust. We get used to it here in Abilene." She turned to face him as he picked up the decanter. "And it has been an unusually dry spring. Still a bit chilly too."

He lifted the brandy, removed the stopper, and tilted the bottle over the empty glass.

He grinned while he was pouring. "I'm from Denver, so this doesn't feel the least bit chilly to me. I suppose I'm accustomed to colder climates. I don't get down this way all that often."

Amanda came over and sat on the edge of a four-post canopy bed. "Like everyone else, I heard the gunshot," she began, with a slow smile crossing her face as she closed the front of her robe to more modest proportions. She had noticed he was looking at the opening. "And I also heard what you said to Justin Davis. I saw you back him down, even though he had a gun in his hand. That takes a great deal of courage. I'm in need of a courageous man.''

He wondered what she meant, why she needed a man who could face a bully like Davis. "I'm afraid I'm not following you. Why do you need a man who isn't afraid of some loudmouthed saloon tough?''

"Davis is more than a saloon tough, Mr. Slocum. He has a very mean reputation. Perhaps you did not know.''

Slocum tasted the brandy and found it to his liking. "I knew all I needed to know, Miss Drake. I've dealt with his kind before. When he's sure he has the upper hand, he'll push it to the limit. The kid he shot was no match for him and he was sure of it all along.''

The warmth left Amanda's face. She stared at Slocum for a moment.

"I hope I didn't say the wrong thing,'' he said, "but I'm all too familiar with the likes of Justin Davis. A reputation with a gun is usually meaningless. A gun can make all men equal, but it still requires guts and knowhow to use one. This Davis knows when to push, and when to back down. He's not stupid. He knew I meant to kill him unless he did exactly what I told him to do, and I think he knew I could get it done.''

"I saw you call his hand,'' Amanda said, reaching for her glass. "I heard most of what you said to him. I was certain he would kill you.''

Slocum grinned. "Plenty of men have tried. Davis had no such intentions. The minute I called his bluff, he behaved just like I figured he would.''

"How did you know? How could you be so sure he wouldn't kill you?''

"His eyes.''

"His eyes?''

"There was fear in 'em.''

At that, Amanda smiled again. "What does fear look like in someone's eyes?''

"They look empty." He sipped more sweet brandy. "I suppose it's more than that. You can tell when another man ain't quite sure of himself."

"By his actions? I'm really curious now."

"It takes a while to learn it. I don't know how to explain it to someone else."

Amanda fixed him with a lingering look. "We don't know each other, Mr. Slocum. I suppose I'm being presumptuous. Let me ask you a very personal question. Would you kill a man . . . if you were well paid for it?"

"No, ma'am, I wouldn't. I'm not a hired gun or any kind of paid assassin."

"You wouldn't?"

"No, ma'am. If that's what you want from me, then you've got the wrong man."

She looked at him demurely over the rim of her goblet. "If the man had it coming?"

Slocum wagged his head. "Like I told you, I'm not a killer for hire."

"I'm disappointed," she said softly, turning down the corners of her mouth.

He rested one foot across his knee. "What has this man done to deserve to die?" he asked.

"He took my sister to Mexico against her will."

"Against her will? You'd better explain."

"He gave her laudanum. She became addicted to it. After a while, she didn't know what she was doing. Then he took her down to the border and I haven't heard from her since. I'm offering a substantial reward for her safe return."

"I think I understand a little better. But you can find the justice you seek with the Texas Rangers. Have you tried?"

She nodded. "I've tried everything. I'm offering men who have courage a reward to cross the Rio Grande to get her back to me safe and sound."

"How much money?" he asked.

"Five thousand dollars in gold."

Slocum's eyebrows knitted. "That's a lot of money. Why are you telling this to me?"

"Because I need help. I need someone who isn't afraid of bad men. My sister is a virtual prisoner. After I heard the gunshot I came to the window. I saw you face down Justin Davis as though it didn't matter who he was, or that he'd just shot a man. You're the sort of man I need to find Alice."

"I don't think I'm followin' you all the way, Miss Drake. You'll pay five thousand dollars to have your sister brought back here? Is that your offer?"

She turned to the window. "Yes. I'll pay five thousand in gold to have her back. No questions will be asked. If you have to break a few laws down in Mexico, I don't care. The man who took her has violated all laws of decency by giving her the drug and now she's helpless."

"Are you absolutely sure she didn't go willingly?"

Amanda tightened her grip on the stem of the goblet. "I am positive of it. I know my sister better than anyone in the whole world."

"I suppose you would."

She relaxed and drank some of her brandy. "He has her and he won't ever let her go."

"I still don't see why the Texas Rangers won't listen to what you have to say."

She took a deep breath. "They have no jurisdiction on the other side of the border."

"That's true enough," he said.

Amanda stared at the floor now. "All I want is to get her back to Abilene, and if you have to kill the man who's holding her prisoner in order to do that, you'll be well paid for it. Five thousand dollars is a lot of money."

Slocum wondered why this pretty woman was living upstairs above a saloon, even one as nice as the Silver Spur.

Her story had a ring of truth to it, if he was any judge of people and honesty. "Before I ask you any more questions, Miss Drake, tell me about your connection to this drinking parlor."

"I own the place," she said.

He grinned, still admiring the subtle curves revealed by her dressing gown. "You don't seem the type to be running a saloon, if you'll pardon the observation."

"Thank you," she whispered. "It's about the last thing on earth I ever wanted to do."

Something about the way Amanda said it made Slocum feel she was sincere. "Why are you making me this offer?" he asked.

She gave him a slightly canted look. "What does it matter if you won't agree to help me?"

He tossed back the contents of his glass and filled it again as he prepared his reply. "I reckon you could say I didn't know all the details."

Her liquid eyes softened some. "If I tell you everything, will you consider helping me, Mr. Slocum?"

"I might. Depends."

"Depends on what?"

"The circumstances. Before you ask me any more questions about whether or not I'll help you, give me some good reasons why I should."

Amanda got off the bed and walked slowly to the window to look down at the street, cradling her brandy goblet against her breast. "I'll have to start from the beginning," she said

"I've got plenty of time," he told her. "All night, if that's how long it takes."

She glanced over her shoulder, a hint of a smile touching her eyes and her mouth. "Was that a proposition, Mr. Slocum?"

He nodded before she settled back on the edge of the bed.

"Tell me where your sister is being kept in Mexico," he said a moment later.

"Laredo. The Mexican town across the river from Laredo. It is called Nuevo Laredo."

Slocum took a deep breath. "I know the city marshal in Laredo. Tom Spence and I have been friends since the war. Tell me more, and while you're at it, pour me another glass of that brandy."

She got up and poured his glass full.

He accepted the drink. "If I agree to help you, which means I'll have to take a train to the Mexican border and leave my horse here in a good stable, how do I know I'll be paid?"

"You'll have to trust me," she said. "First, listen to what I have to say, the story of my sister and this horrible man who was hired by a Mexican bandit to introduce her to the opiates. He came to Abilene, calling himself Carl Smith, dressed in fancy clothes, pretending to court my sister. He gave her very small amounts of laudanum at first, until she was addicted. Then he spirited her away one night and took her to Mexico, to the evil man who'd hired him. Now she's a prisoner there, drugged on laudanum, and this Mexican friend intends to keep her that way, making her his sex slave. There's more I can tell you. Then you can decide if you are willing to take the train to Laredo. Just hear me out. I have a feeling that once you've heard the whole story, you'll agree to help me. And I'll tell you this much more. I'll pay you five thousand dollars if you bring Alice back to Abilene, and I'll have my bank here transfer five thousand in gold to Laredo, to be offered as ransom for my sister. You'll be carrying a letter from the Laredo bank authorizing the withdrawal on your signature. Are you interested now, Mr. Slocum?''

"You have my undivided attention, Miss Drake. Tell me every detail, everything you know about your sister's abduction.''

4

A slender brunette girl, only three weeks from her twentieth birthday, lay atop a four-poster bed, her wrists and ankles tied to the bedposts. In pale lamplight the bearded man towering over her brandishing a long bowie knife seemed demonic, an evil thing, his face twisted into a network of deep lines etched in a leathery mask of skin the color of creamed coffee. A black beard clung to his cheeks and chin in twists and curls that were matted in tight little knots. When he grinned cruelly, a gold tooth at the front of his mouth caught reflected glow from a lantern on a table beside the bed. Alice Drake lay stunned, barely able to move, spread-eagled on a stained, foul-smelling mattress. She watched Luis Zambrano undress her with his eyes when his obsidian orbs drifted across her body, pausing at her breasts, then on the cleft of her thighs. Her blue gingham dress was torn after she'd been tied across the back of a horse for the ride deep into Mexico. And now, as Zambrano stared at the buttons down the front of her thin summer gown, she opened her mouth to scream, for she knew he meant to cut her clothes off and use her body.

"Be silent, brown-haired bitch," he growled in Spanish, "or I will hit you again!" He had delivered a clubbing blow to her face just moments earlier when she'd cried out while her hands and feet were being tied to the bed. Blood trickled from one corner of her mouth, running down her porcelain cheek to a pillow below her head. The dose of laudanum he had given her seemed to have very little effect.

Zambrano looked over his shoulder. A *pistolero* with two bandoliers crisscrossing his chest stood near the door with a rifle. "Leave us alone, Juanito," Zambrano commanded. "Shoot anyone who comes near the adobe. Tell Ortiz to make sure the men have plenty of tequila while I teach this gringo bitch how to make love to a man."

"*Sí, Jefe,*" Juanito said, opening a thin plank door for a look outside. He grinned when he cast a backwards glance at the girl. "She is a beautiful woman, the most beautiful woman I have ever seen. Perhaps she is a virgin? If I hear her screaming I will know. . . ."

"Get out!" Zambrano snapped, returning his attention to the girl. He lowered the tip of his knife blade to the top button on her dress and sliced it off. When the button fell he laughed and cut off another button, then one more, until the front of her dress fell open, revealing a lace bodice gathered at the front by a cotton cord. He sliced the cord in half, the tip of his knife making a tearing sound. The girl gasped, eyes rounding with fear when Zambrano bent over her to cup one small, firm breast in a calloused hand.

"Do not scream," he shouted in thickly accented English, "or I will cut your throat! Be silent if you wish to live to see the sun rise again." He placed the tip of his knife to her neck so it pricked her skin, drawing a trace of blood. Then he squeezed her breast, pinching her nipple between his thumb and forefinger. Alice squirmed, but she made no sound even when he increased pressure around her rosy pink nipple while the knife was held to her windpipe. Tears flooded her eyes. Her arms and legs trembled.

Her tongue flicked out to catch some of the blood running from her lips, and when Zambrano saw this, he laughed. "Stupid *puta*!" he cried. "You are nothing but a white man's whore! Damn you! Stop your whimpering!"

Alice closed her eyes. Everything seemed like a bad dream. The stairs to the bedroom were guarded by four gun-wielding bandits. She was a prisoner of the leader of the gang whom the others called Zambrano, a loathsome giant with an oily unwashed smell. As he bent over her now, his breath reeking of liquor, Alice understood what he was about to do to her. He intended to have his way with her, and if she fought him he might kill her. The lau- danum he had given her when they first came to Nuevo Laredo made her sleepy, but not too sleepy to know what was about to happen next.

She felt him knead her breast roughly, causing more pain, although she could not open her eyes. A series of tremors raced down her arms and legs. She flinched when something touched the top of her underwear, the cold steel of Zambrano's knife blade. A ripping sound startled her when her undergarment was torn from her hips. She lay naked, stretched out on the bed, her mound and breasts exposed, tattered remnants of her dress lying around her. The moment was at hand and she knew this, even though she had not ever been with a man—until now.

Zambrano grunted, and through slitted eyelids Alice saw him unfasten his pants. As he pulled them off his hips, his cock stood erect, pulsing with blood. Alice had never seen a prick so large. A few times she'd witnessed a *vaquero* urinating behind the barn when she came around a corner too quietly. But in all her life she had never seen a cock so thick or so long, blunted at the head, much too large to enter her without causing terrible agony or tearing her tender flesh.

The bed shook when Zambrano came between her parted

thighs, and his foul smell threatened to overwhelm her. She drew back against the mattress as far as she could, and held her breath for the moment when he thrust himself inside her. She caught a brief glimpse of the knife in his hand. He squeezed her right breast harder until it was all she could do to stifle a cry by pressing her lips together.

"Lie very still, *mi hita*," he warned, lowering his body over hers. His tremendous weight almost crushed her, and for a moment she feared she would not be able to breathe.

A soft whimper escaped her mouth despite her best efforts to silence it. She felt the head of his cock touch the hair of her mound. She was surprised to find herself wet, the way she got at night when she allowed herself to dream about what making love to a man would be like. It infuriated her that she would get wet at a time like this, with a man so repulsive, so revolting. Why was she so aroused by being taken against her will?

His powerful hand crushed her breast, squeezing her flesh in a vise-like grip. It was all she could do to keep from screaming as a fresh wave of tears filled her eyes. But the most excruciating pain she had ever known followed immediately thereafter, as the head of Zambrano's cock pushed the lips of her cunt apart. Alice gasped, eyes bulging wide. "No!" she cried, shaking her head back and forth atop the pillow. "Please . . . don't do this to me!"

He answered her with a cruel laugh, shoving his prick deeper inside her. Pain radiated from her mound like chains of lightning in a thunderstorm, crackling with intensity. Her abdomen shook violently, her thighs quivering while she tried desperately to pull away from his rock-hard member. It felt as if something was being torn inside her.

"It will feel good," he whispered hoarsely, his lips close to her ear. "Tonight you will become a woman. . . ."

Again, he thrust himself deeper into her cunt, and when she felt the girth of his prick, she screamed at the top of her lungs until it seemed the rafters above the bed trembled. Before her scream died in her throat, he struck her with an open palm and the force of the blow sent her mind reeling. Winking stars appeared before her eyes—she tasted fresh blood and her left cheek ached with a thousand bee stings. She struggled against her restraints uselessly, hoping to free her arms. Another cry came involuntarily from deep in her chest, a cry of pain and humiliation she could not suppress.

"Shut up, bitch!" Zambrano snarled, leering down at her. He thrust his hips downward, sending another inch of cock into her moist cunt. Renewed pain in her groin made her forget about the vicious blow to her face. Her head lolled to one side, and she lay still in a state of shock while more of his prick was pushed inside her. It felt as if a tree trunk was wedged between the lips of her mound. The girth of his shaft made her feel as if she would explode, or split in two halves. She fought back more tears—this filthy bandit was taking her virginity and she would never be the same again. No decent man would ever want her for a wife after tonight. Her life would be ruined.

Only seconds later he began to thrust back and forth, in and out of her, in a short, jerky motion. Alice could hear the wet juices in her cunt making a sucking noise when he pulled back for another deep thrust into her womb. She wanted to scream each time his length penetrated her, yet she knew it would only anger him—he would hit her again. It was utterly useless to resist.

Zambrano began to pant with exertion. Sweat beaded on his face and neck, his chest. The bed squeaked each time he rocked forward and his terrible smell increased, the odor of sweat and tequila. He placed his knife on the pillow beside her head in order to grab a fistful of her hair. Thrusting, panting, he made each penetration harder, more forceful, until the full weight of his groin hammered against her stomach.

"Please," she whimpered softly, "don't hurt me."

His breath came in ragged bursts now and his thrusts quickened. The wet sound her cunt grew louder, as his cock sucked her juices out when his shaft withdrew. And as the tempo of his thrusting increased, a strange new sensation hinting at pleasure started in Alice's womb. She resisted it with all her might, embarrassed by it. Why would it feel good to have a man take her by force? It wasn't possible, and yet a warm feeling had begun inside her . . . or was she only imagining it?

Zambrano grunted each time his cock slammed into her cunt. He was sweating profusely, trembling with desire, and noises made by the squeaking bed were louder, more distinct.

"Please don't hurt me," Alice groaned, enveloped by a new feeling, a bewildering combination of pleasure and pain.

The rhythm of his thrusts became faster. Wet sucking sounds accompanied each movement he made, and he gasped for air. Along with the increase in his heavy breathing, his hips gyrated downward more forcefully. Soon, Alice's cunt felt on fire with sensations she never knew she had. In a way she could not explain, it felt as if she were about to explode. She was not thinking about Zambrano's smell or his sweat trickling down onto her naked body. Something about the experience had changed, and it was not altogether unpleasant.

She found herself meeting his thrusts with her own, before she realized what she was doing. Some frenetic energy had taken over her actions, and now they were beyond her control. Arching her spine, she drove her mound against his shaft with a rhythm equal to his and while she did this, more of the warm tingling spread through her cunt.

"You like it, gringo bitch!" Zambrano said.

Had she been able, she would have denied it, yet for now

the pleasure almost outweighed the pain and she found she was unable to speak.

"Tell me you like it!" he shouted, drawing his lips back over his teeth, a demand Alice didn't fully comprehend in the throes of his passion.

"No!" she hissed, unwilling to give in to him at a time like this, forced against her will to do his bidding.

His fist knotted more deeply into her brown hair. He gave a jerk with his hand, awakening her to a new form of pain when her scalp began to hurt.

"Tell me you like it!" he cried again.

It did seem her pleasure heightened somewhat, but she would rather have died than admit this to him now. "No," she whimpered quietly, protesting as much as she dared.

He slapped her, harder than before, and she almost lost consciousness. Her mouth filled with blood, and she noticed a cut on her lower lip after she ran her tongue across it. When she tried to speak the words came out garbled, indistinct, like she spoke jibberish.

Then a sudden burst of sensation overtook her, the warmth of something deep within her groin gaining intensity. Her pelvis rocked against Zambrano's cock frantically in spite of the hurt and embarrassment she felt. She strained every muscle in her body, and her limbs turned to iron. She trembled and let out a cry that was animal-like, not of her own making. Her womb convulsed. As the sensation grew she let herself go, no longer fighting it as she had before.

Zambrano shuddered. A flood of warm wetness spilled from his testicles. Pumping, grunting, gasping for air, he sent his seed into her belly in a series of mighty thrusts. He groaned as his jism flowed, and for a moment he went rigid, straining, a look of ecstasy on his face. Seconds later he collapsed on top of her completely spent.

Alice found she was unable to breathe with his heavy body on top of hers. He was crushing her, and yet there was something about the experience that was curiously enjoyable.

"You . . . are . . . too . . . heavy," she gasped, squirming underneath him.

He did not seem to hear her.

"Please get off . . . of me," she begged, turning to one side so his weight was less oppressive.

Zambrano's eyes batted open. He stared down at her for a time while, still breathing hard, drops of sweat dripping off his cheeks and a few tiny hairs at the end of his beard.

She felt his cock soften inside her, and that was when the realization struck her that she was no longer truly whole. She had given up her virginity at knifepoint to a Mexican bandit, and the thought of what she had done left her feeling empty, alone. It wasn't that she'd had a choice, for she was certain that her life hung in the balance. But now, as the moment passed, she began to experience deepening sorrow. The laudanum softened the sting of what she had done . . . what she had allowed him to do.

She gazed up at the ceiling. At least she was alive, and if the opportunity came, she might be able to escape the clutches of Zambrano and get back to her sister's place in Texas. She told herself that patience was necessary, awaiting the right opportunity. Until then, she must do whatever it took to stay alive, hoping Amanda would understand.

5

Slocum propped his boots on the iron veranda railing and lit a rum-soaked cheroot. He tasted sweet smoke, and gave a contented sigh before picking up his brandy snifter. Good brandy was hard to find in San Antonio; only the best places, like here at the Saint Anthony Hotel, offered quality liquors and fine cigars. It was one reason he hired a room here whenever he was in San Antone on business. Or pleasure. Glancing over his shoulder past the French doors into his suite, he briefly considered the abundance of pleasure he'd found on this trip. Pleasure had come in the form of a woman last night, as his pleasures so often did. Ellen was quite a woman. He saw her sleeping below a lace canopy above the bed, and the sight brought him sweet recollections of the previous evening. Her soft cries of passion had been just what he needed after a long train ride in blistering summer heat from Abilene to San Antonio. As a crimson sunrise greeted him this morning, he thought about the arrangement he'd made with Amanda Drake, and the promise of what was to come if he were successful, not just the five thousand dollars, but a chance to bed her.

His meeting with Amanda regarding the Mexican bandit who held her sister prisoner had taken him by surprise.

He'd wired Laredo City Marshal Tom Spence that he was on his way down. Years earlier, Tom had sent him across the border looking for the daughter of a rich Laredo rancher who had been kidnapped by a ruthless revolutionary outlaw named Victoriano Valdez. Back then, Slocum had risked his life for a ten-thousand-dollar reward. And now the mention of a five-thousand-dollar reward was no small matter. If Tom said there there might be big trouble locating a bandit named Luis Zambrano in Mexico, it was information Slocum trusted. He and Tom had served together in the Army of Virginia during the worst years of the war, and they knew each other well, having fought side by side at Bull Run and later as a part of Pickett's Charge under the command of Stonewall Jackson. Sharing that brutal war experience had made Slocum and Tom fast friends, although they hadn't seen each other for years now. Tom's wire had simply said he'd be glad to help all he could.

Slocum wondered about the sister in Mexico. According to Amanda's story, Alice Drake had been drugged and then taken across the river, where another revolution was in the making. Slocum knew little about all the troubles going on in Mexico beyond reports he'd read in the newspapers. Revolution was always brewing down there, and all manner of men from the States were hiring out as mercenaries to help bring down what was widely reported to be a corrupt government in Mexico City. But these revolutionary bands were said to be a mix of lawless *pistoleros* and dedicated patriots. It was hard to tell one bunch from another, so the stories went. But for a princely sum like five thousand dollars, Slocum knew he was willing to take a few calculated risks in order to find out if the girl could be freed. Making discreet inquiries seldom got too dangerous if a man knew what he was about and watched his backside closely.

He took a puff from his cheroot and let the smoke lift in lazy swirls on a breath of warm morning wind. He'd be boarding a train for Laredo before noon, and by tomorrow he would know more about the girl's abduction. Only then would he decide if there were a chance to successfully arrange for the release of Alice Drake. Until then he would think about the five thousand and how he could spend it, a nice way to pass a few morning hours. Then there was the promise of a night in Amanda's bed, if he brought Alice back unharmed.

A soft knock on the door announced the arrival of their food, and he got up to let the waiter in. Having breakfast sent up to his room was something he regularly did while staying at the Saint Anthony, in part because of the wonderful view his room usually had of the city and the San Antonio River. Granted it was a luxury he rarely afforded himself otherwise, but a stay in San Antone was special, restful, good tonic for his nerves from time to time after business elsewhere.

As a precaution he touched the butt of the small bellygun he carried inside his shirt before opening the door. The little .32-caliber Colt had saved his life a number of times. Being careful was so much a part of his nature now that he rarely ever gave any thought to it. While he usually relied on a .44/.40 Peacemaker revolver when trouble came his way, he still carried the bellygun on most occasions. At close quarters the .32 was deadly if a man could hit what he was aiming at with a short-barrel pistol.

He opened the door a crack and found a waiter balancing a tray standing in the hallway. The aroma of fresh coffee and the scent of fried bacon made Slocum's mouth water. "Bring it in," he said quietly. "Try not to disturb the lady sleeping in the next room."

There was something about Slocum's admonition that gave the young Mexican waiter pause, but after a moment of hesitation he came in and set the tray down on a polished mahogany table at the center of the room. Slocum tipped the boy a silver two-bit piece, and waited until he closed the door behind him. Pouring coffee into a white china cup, he added a splash of brandy. Underneath a silver serving cover he found strips of bacon and slices of ham in a dish surrounded by scrambled eggs. A wicker basket of biscuits was covered by a linen cloth. Bowls of strawberry jam and butter rounded out their meal.

Carrying his spiked coffee, he entered the bedroom. Ellen slept on her back, magnificent breasts jutting from her rib cage like snowcapped mountains. Her blond curls lay across a pillow in disarray, framing her round face. A bedsheet lay over her stomach, barely covering her from the waist down, and for a time he simply stood there, admiring her physical beauty. He'd known her for a number of years, and it seemed as the years passed she only got prettier. He judged she was close to thirty by now; however, her age didn't show in ways he noticed. She became a fiery demon in bed after a couple bottles of champagne, and no matter how many times he bedded her, he always found it most satisfying. She was one of those rare women who couldn't be fulfilled by a single act of lovemaking. Last night she had demanded that he take her again and again, until at last she'd drifted off to sleep. Perhaps this was one reason why he'd grown so fond of her. Ellen had an insatiable appetite for prick. When he entered her, she came to a climax almost at once, and from that moment on she became one of the most sensual women he'd ever known in bed.

A breeze lifted lace curtains away from a bedroom window, and let them drop against the windowsill when the breath of wind died down. Ellen stirred, making a tiny fist with one hand to rub her eyes. It was then Slocum noticed her other hand covered by the sheet, and the slow circular motion she made with two fingers she'd inserted into her cunt while still asleep. Her pelvis began to grind unconsciously against the pressure of her fingers, and she gave a soft moan of pleasure.

"She's still hot," Slocum whispered in disbelief. They had made love for hours last night, and yet she still wanted more. He found it amazing that any woman could require so much stimulation. Ellen was quite a woman, more than most men could satisfy. That, he supposed, was what intrigued him about her. He watched her fingers move faster across the lips of her cunt. Muscles in her legs tightened. He wondered how she could remain asleep when desire overtook her like this.

A slow smile crossed her face. Her eyelids parted ever so slightly. "You've been watching me," she said huskily. "You thought I was still sleeping, didn't you? How can a woman sleep with a handsome man in the same room? Come to bed, John, and I'll show you how a woman should treat a man first thing in the morning."

"Our breakfast is here, Ellen. Aren't you hungry?"

She giggled quietly, playfully. "Hungry for more of your stiff cock, Mr. Slocum." She threw the sheet aside to reveal her cunt and the location of her fingers.

"Our eggs will get cold. . . ."

"To hell with our eggs. I want to feel your balls against my buttocks. We can have eggs another time."

He took another sip of laced coffee and grinned. "You're some woman, Ellen. I did my best last night, and now you're after more. Remember, I've got a train to catch."

"Come to me, John," she whispered, beckoning to him with wet fingers she withdrew from her cunt. "Make love to me, and do it hard this time. I want something to remember you by. It's too long between your visits to San Antone."

He put his cup down and began unbuttoning his shirt. Seeing her naked, begging him to make love to her, he felt an erection begin to pulse inside his pants. Shouldering out of his shirt, he let it fall on the edge of the bed before unfastening his trousers. All the while, Ellen continued to rub her fingers around the lips of her mound, moaning softly.

He lay between her milky thighs and licked one pink nipple with the tip of his tongue, then placed it in his mouth and started to suck on it noisily.

"Oh, John!" Ellen cried, twisting underneath him, placing her heels behind his knees to draw him close. She reached for his cock and stroked it a few times, until passion got the best of her. She put the head between her moist lips and arched her back while pulling him by the hips. His cock entered her pussy, and at once she began feverishly hunching against the base of his shaft, taking every inch of him inside her. She dug her fingernails into the skin of his back and emitted a moan of pure pleasure, rocking under him, squirming, breathing harder and harder.

He took her roughly this time, without any of the gentle attention he'd given her last night. He drove his prick into her as hard as he could, and their bodies slammed together with increasing frequency until the canopy above the bed shook. Summoning all his power, he stabbed his cock into her cunt as if it were a weapon.

When she reached her release, she let out a wail that he was sure could be heard in the hallway. Her body trembled, frozen in a moment of ecstasy until her climax ebbed away. At last she fell back on the sheet, completely spent, but he was not finished with her yet. Stroking harder, faster, he reached his own climax a moment later, and stiffened when his balls emptied in her womb.

When he looked down at Ellen, her eyes were glazed over. She smiled. "That was what I wanted, darling John. Something I can remember during those lonely nights while you're away so long."

• • •

He climbed aboard the passenger car with his valise and war bag under his arm. He waved to Ellen as the locomotive whistle sounded. She returned his wave, tilting her black parasol so he could see her face clearly. The black dress she wore revealed so much cleavage that other passengers couldn't help but stare when they walked past.

Slocum turned into the car and started down a narrow aisle to find a seat, briefly noting faces of other passengers along the way to see if he recognized anyone. It was born out of old habit. He always entered a strange place with the same amount of care, to make certain no one waited for him there who might have an old score to settle.

He found a seat at the rear of the car and put his belongings in a rack above him. He noted that several passengers were watching him, paying attention to his gunbelt and the cross-pull holster he wore underneath his black split-tail frock coat. Not many men employed a cross-pull rig for their side arms, and he had grown accustomed to a few stares. One gent in particular, a man wearing a brown derby hat and silk vest seated across the aisle, paid more attention to his gun than usual. Slocum settled into his seat and glanced out a window, until the stranger's stares lasted too long. He turned across the aisle. "What the hell are you looking at, mister?"

The stranger's face did not change, nor did he seem put off by Slocum's tone or the question. "Your gun," he replied. "I don't see many belly-draw contraptions in my line of work. Just call it simple curiosity."

There was something about this stranger Slocum didn't like. "Too damn much curiosity to be polite," Slocum said tonelessly. "I'd hate like hell to have to teach you better manners before this train pulls out."

Again, there was no change in the man's expression, no show of fear over Slocum's threat. "That might wind up bein' a tall order, pardner. I figure you believe yourself to be pretty good with that gun or you wouldn't talk so big. In case you're of a mind to wonder, I'm a right decent shot myself. Unless you're willing to find out who's the better shot, I'd keep those lessons in manners to myself.''

Slocum noticed the bulge of a gun inside the stranger's coat hanging in a shoulder holster. However, the challenge was not the kind of thing he could ignore. Several passengers seated around them overheard what was being said and fell silent, watching the exchange. Slocum grinned at the man across the aisle. In the same instant his right hand jerked his Peacemaker free with a single fluid motion. He sprang from his seat, aiming into the space between the stranger's eyes—the man was reaching for his pistol when he heard the click of Slocum's Colt being cocked a few inches from his skull. His hand froze.

"You're too damn slow," Slocum hissed. "Now hand me your gun butt-first or I'll blow a tunnel through your head. One wrong move and somebody'll be scooping up your brains from that platform outside."

"Jesus," the stranger croaked, swallowing, staring into the dark muzzle of Slocum's .44/.40. "Don't shoot me, mister. I was only havin' a little fun." Very carefully he lifted a small-bore revolver from his coat with thumb and forefinger, holding it out so Slocum could take it. Passengers throughout the noisy car had ended their conversations to watch what was taking place.

Slocum seized the gun and stuck it in his belt. Slowly he began to relax, realizing that his temper had gotten the best of him. He let the hammer down on his Peacemaker and straightened up, glancing along the aisle. "Trouble's over, folks," he said. "Just a little misunderstanding." He turned back to the stranger and holstered his Colt. "Having a little fun almost cost you your life, mister. If it was me, I'd remember that the next time I found myself in the mood for some fun, 'cause it damn near got you killed." Slocum took a deep breath to calm his nerves. "I want your name, mister, and then tell me about this line of work you say you're in having to do with guns."

"I'm Cabe McAlister," he said quietly. "I'm headed down to Laredo to look for a wanted man. There's a reward posted. . . ."

"I know all about rewards," Slocum told him, mildly surprised to learn that McAlister was traveling to Laredo with the same objective as his own. "I'll be looking for a wanted man myself. The city marshal at Laredo is a friend of mine. Tom wired me to come down. I've got some advice for you, Mr. McAlister, and I suggest you pay real close attention to it. Don't get in my way down there, or the next time I won't let you off so easy. Stay clear of me or you might not live to regret it."

Slocum sat back down, his anger cooling.

"Sorry," McAlister said, turning his face to a window. He slumped in his seat just as the locomotive began to chug away from the depot.

Slocum felt the other passengers staring at him after the confrontation. He had allowed his temper to get out of hand at the wrong time. It would be a long train ride to Laredo with so many people afraid of him now.

As the depot fell away behind the train, Slocum put his mind on other matters; the captive girl in Mexico, and seeing his old friend Tom Spence again. Only once did he consider that McAlister was a bounty hunter, or that more men of his ilk were likely to show up around Laredo looking for a chance to earn big rewards looking for wanted men. Men like McAlister would only get in the way, and there was even a risk they might make all the Mexican bandits wary. Slocum knew big money would attract all sorts of desperate men hoping to make a payday.

He watched the outskirts of San Antonio pass by the window as the locomotive chugged away from town. From the corner of his eye he saw McAlister get up and move to another seat to be farther away from him for the long ride to the border. A lesson in better manners had done him a world of good.

Slocum settled back against his seat, looking forward to seeing Tom Spence again after so many years. They'd had rough times together during the war, and Slocum was sure Tom remembered them as well as he did.

6

Slocum slumped against the back of the swaying seat, listening to the rhythmic click of train wheels crossing section joints in the tracks, remembering Tom Spence and the war. A hot, sooty wind blew in his face from the passenger car window. He paid no attention to mile after empty mile of mesquite brushland through which the train labored, for his mind was elsewhere, back to a bloody battle at Manassas where he'd first met Tom, a boy about the same age as he, barely seventeen.

Although they both served in the Calhoun County Militia, they were from different parts of the Allegheny Mountains and hadn't met until the militia, commanded by John's father, William Slocum, was called to war when the state of Georgia joined other secessionist states in the summer of 1860. John's older brother, Robert, rode off with them to fight Yankees. Their father lost his life to a minie ball he took at Manassas. Robert was killed in 1863, just after being commissioned a lieutenant in a charge led by Thomas "Stonewall" Jackson. Jackson earned his nickname at Manassas, called the battle of Bull Run. Jackson's Brigade was known throughout the Confederacy for its courage, a reputation that probably cost Robert Slocum his life.

Robert was at the front of Pickett's Charge in the battle for Little Round Top at Gettysburg. John was assigned to the sharpshooters covering the charge, and that fact—that he was a superior marksman, had most likely been the reason his life was spared that fateful day at Gettysburg. With a Spencer rifle he'd taken off a dead Yankee, his aim was almost perfect. Fighting alongside him, young Tom Spence was also a crack shot, cutting down men in blue as fast as he could reload. After that terrible experience he and Tom were all but inseparable, until General Lee made John a courier to General Sterling Price after Grant's victory at Vicksburg.

Now that the Union controlled the Mississippi, General Price had to fight a different war in the west. "Bloody Kansas," as it was called, had been turned into a bloody battleground by Union Jayhawkers and Confederate Redlegs. Quantrill led a band of Confederates so ruthless that Richmond severed relations with them. Burning and looting became so commonplace that neither side observed a code of honor. John was promoted to the rank of captain by General Price, who assigned him to Quantrill.

It was with the madman Quantrill that John Slocum learned mastery of the Colt revolver, and also where he developed an attitude toward fighting and death that was to become a part of his nature for the balance of his lifetime. When he was with Quantrill at Lawrence, Kansas, Slocum caught a bullet that nearly killed him. It was months later, in the spring of 1866, after the war ended, before Slocum was well enough to travel, returning home to find his father and mother both dead, his farm seized for back taxes by the new carpetbagger government in Reconstruction Georgia. At the family farm he killed his first men out of uniform, a gunman hired to enforce carpetbagger policies in Calhoun County and the county judge who came to serve papers on the Slocum farm. With warrants out for his arrest,

Slocum had put a torch to the place and ridden west to escape bitter memories and a death sentence.

The passenger car rocked, awakening Slocum from thoughts of his past. He stared out the window, thinking about Tom Spence and a happy reunion when he got to Laredo. If Tom wanted, they might talk about the war for a while, but if Slocum had his way they wouldn't discuss it. It was a time he wanted to forget. The war had cost him his family and their homestead, and given him a terrible scar as a reminder of how close he'd come to death. He remembered reading somewhere that over 600,000 men had died on both sides—he'd seen the bloated corpses at Manassas and in the Shenandoah Valley, and finally at Gettysburg. It made no sense to talk about what they'd seen back then, what they'd gone through together. Slocum was sure Tom remembered it as vividly as he did. It occasionally robbed Slocum of sleep when dreams about those times awakened him in a cold sweat.

The train slowed near a water tower in the midst of a bald mesquite prairie to take on water and firewood for the boiler. A clapboard shack sat beside the tracks and behind it, an old wagon drawn by a rawboned gray mule sat in the shade of an eave. A boy in white cotton pants waited for the train to stop. He carried a box of sandwiches and a masonry jar advertising "lemonade." As soon as the locomotive ground to a halt, the boy climbed into the first passenger car to peddle his wares. Passengers got up to stretch and make use of a small two-door outhouse behind the shack. But as Slocum was coming to his feet, he saw McAlister coming over and by the look on his face, there was something on his mind.

"Look, mister, I'm powerful sorry for what I said a while ago," McAlister began. "I'd sure like to get my gun back, if it's all the same to you."

Slocum's eyes narrowed. "What'll keep you from trying your luck again, maybe when my back's turned?"

"You've got my word I won't do no such thing," he replied, eyes darting to the butt of his pistol stuck in the waistband of Slocum's pants.

"Why would I think your word is any good, McAlister? You don't strike me as any kind of honorable man. You wanted to goad me into a gunfight when I got on this train. . . ."

"I gave you an honest apology for that. There ain't a hell of a lot more a man can do besides give his word."

Slocum was still sizing him up. "I'll think on it some," he said, sounding doubtful.

McAlister appeared to be encouraged. "Maybe the two of us can strike a bargain of some kind, maybe go in partners to look for outlaws down in Mexico, split the rewards two ways."

"I always work alone, Mr. McAlister. Besides, as slow as you are going for your gun, you probably wouldn't live long down below the border. That neck of the woods is full of hard cases who'd blow your brains out for the boots you're wearing. I've spent some time down in Tamaulipas and Coahuila. There's a man on damn near every street corner who'd kill you for the price of a jug of tequila. Forget about us forming any sort of partnership. It ain't in my deck of cards."

Now McAlister was a little put off. "You ain't had a chance to see what I can do, mister. I can read hoofprints the way some men read a newspaper, an' I'm something of an expert on explosives if I do say so myself. I've got some dynamite packed in a box in the baggage car. Dynamite is liable to come in real handy if you find the owlhoots you're lookin' for holed up some place."

Slocum frowned. "Dynamite could also kill innocent folks."

"Not if the man who uses it knows what he's doin'. I got a lot of experience workin' with explosives. I done the dynamitin' for several mining companies in Colorado. I know how to make a hole in solid rock the size of a man's head, or I can bring down half a mountain if I take a mind to. If those outlaws take a notion to fortify themselves someplace, dynamite's the only way to blast 'em out. And I know how to use a rifle. I've made a pretty fair livin' huntin' down wanted men in the territories of late."

"You're a bounty hunter," Slocum observed dryly, having a dislike for men of his persuasion.

"Some call it that," McAlister agreed. "I go after men the law can't find themselves. I'm usually pretty successful at it."

"You're damn sure slow on the draw," Slocum remembered.

"Never claimed to be no professional shootist. I had you figured for a gambler, by the cut of your fancy suit. I got no use for cardsharps, an' that's what you looked like to me. I said I was sorry for what I said, for what happened. I was wrong. I misjudged you."

It was a risk, but Slocum took out McAlister's pistol and handed it back to him butt-first. "You can keep your gun, but if you reach for it again when I'm around, I swear I'll kill you dead as a fence post."

McAlister took his revolver and returned it to his shoulder holster. "What about the chances of a partnership between you an' me? Two sets of eyes are better'n one."

"I'll think on it some, but I'd call it highly unlikely. I told you before that I work alone."

"I'd carry my share of the load. We'd make a good team, you an' me."

"I doubt it," Slocum remarked, "but you're entitled to your opinion."

McAlister glanced over his shoulder as the boy selling

food and drinks came down the aisle. "Let me buy you a sandwich and a glass of lemonade. We'll talk over lunch."

Slocum shook his head. "No, thanks. I never drink lemonade, and I'm not in the habit of eating with strangers who try to pull a gun on me."

"I said I was sorry 'bout that. I had you figured wrong."

"After I have a talk with Marshal Spence at Laredo I'll know more about what I'm up against. If I think there's any need for a man who knows explosives, I'll look you up. Until then, consider the matter closed. I'm not looking for any partners."

McAlister's face fell as Slocum turned to leave the train to stretch his legs. Slocum knew it was a gamble, turning his back on a man who'd gone for a gun against him a few hours ago, but he had McAlister judged for a cowardly man who wouldn't take another chance like that unless he was convinced he couldn't lose.

When Slocum climbed down from the car, he gave the surrounding dry brushland a passing examination. Everything that grew in south Texas had thorns. Slender mesquite trees had razor-like spines on every branch, and beds of cactus lying everywhere were bristling with needles. Rare tufts of dry buffalo grass grew in small clumps between the mesquites and cactus. It was a no-man's land if ever there was one, and this was what most of northern Mexico was like. The ground was powder-dry. Water for men and horses would be scarce. Without knowledge of where to find rare waterholes, a man could die of thirst in a matter of days.

He sauntered over to the woodshed and rested in the shade to escape a blistering sun blazing down on the railroad stop. He wondered how he would fare crossing land like this on the back of a horse. It would be one hell of a test of horseflesh, requiring that he purchase a range-bred animal wise to the ways of a desert. Tom could help him with that. If Slocum decided to go at all. It would depend on what he could learn about the bandits' territory and the places they were known to frequent. Without getting good information ahead of time, he would be looking for a needle in a haystack down there.

He watched trainmen drain water from the wooden tower into the belly of the locomotive. Without precious water not even a train could manage this brutal land. A well or a river would be the lifeblood those bandits needed. Learning where to find water in the region he had to cross was his first order of business if he agreed to take the job.

He thought back to McAlister. McAlister was untrustworthy, Slocum was sure of that. But a time might come when a man who knew explosives could come in handy. On a few occasions in the past, Slocum had made deals with the Devil's own representatives in order to accomplish his objectives.

The train whistle sounded, announcing time for passengers to reboard. He pushed away from the woodshed wall and walked slowly back to the car. According to a conductor, they should make it to Laredo before midnight if the locomotive or loose tracks didn't give any unforseen delays.

Slocum took his seat by a rear window, after sleeving out of his coat to escape the sweltering heat. He laid his coat beside him and tilted his hat over his eyes, making sure McAlister was in another part of the car. Earlier, Slocum had noticed a young woman aboard the train, a brunette with rouge on her cheeks and painted red lips. She wore a gray gown buttoned high on her neck, presenting a very proper and ladylike appearance. But once in a while he caught her staring at him, although she always looked away quickly when their eyes met. She was a pretty woman and given the chance, he would have liked to get to know her.

The locomotive belched steam and slowly chugged away from the water tower. Keeping his hat brim low over his eyes, Slocum admired the woman in secret, the swell of her breasts inside her dress and the delicate curve of her ankles where her stockings showed beneath the hem of her gown. Soon the train labored to full speed, pounding its way south amid a cloud of black soot pouring from the smokestack.

Later, Slocum noticed the woman take out a paper fan and begin fanning herself. The seat beside her was vacant, and he pondered his chances of joining her in the empty seat. But if she had witnessed the exchange between himself and McAlister, it was unlikely she would invite him to sit beside her. It was an unfortunate incident, but one that couldn't be helped.

Two hours later the sun set to the west, allowing cooler air into the windows of the car. The pretty brunette put her fan away and adjusted her skirt across the hardwood seat. Then she looked up at Slocum and caught him watching her. She gave him a slight smile and a polite nod before she looked the other way.

"I might get lucky," he whispered to himself. Her smile had been an outright invitation, he thought.

A few more minutes passed before Slocum put on his coat and tugged down the cuffs of his sleeves, making himself as presentable as possible. He stood up and reached into his valise for a pint of good Kentucky whiskey he'd purchased for the trip. If he offered the lady a drink, he hoped she wouldn't be offended. . . .

7

The interior of the car had begun to darken after sunset as
Slocum made his way up the gently rocking aisle carrying
his pint of sour mash whiskey. He paused in front of the
woman and tipped his hat, giving her a friendly grin.

"A pleasant evening, ma'am. I wondered if you might
care to join me in a drink of bourbon. I hope I'm not being
too forward. Allow me to introduce myself. My name is
John Slocum. Would you care for a drink?"

She had been watching him from the moment he left his
seat. A look of concern crossed her face, then disappeared.
"I do not usually imbibe with strangers, Mr. Slocum. I was
a witness to that rather ugly incident with the other passenger, and I must say that you seem to be quite a rogue. It
hardly seems proper for a woman of good breeding to sit
and drink liquor with a total stranger who threatened another passenger with a pistol."

Slocum liked the sound of her voice. "That was an unfortunate occurrence, one that I sincerely regret. However,
the man was insisting upon a confrontation. I never meant
to shoot him, only to teach him some better manners. I can
assure that I'm not the rogue you think I am. Given the
opportunity, I feel sure I can convince you otherwise."

A playful smile lifted the corners of her ruby lips. "I may have been wrong about you, Mr. Slocum. My name is Etta Willingham. I'm a schoolteacher on my way to a teaching assignment in Laredo at the Normal School for Girls. I suppose no harm will come from sharing a small drink with you. Please do sit down."

He accepted her invitation, and took a seat opposite hers as the conductor came into the car lighting oil lamps. A few of the other passengers watched him sit down with the woman, including Cabe McAlister, although they turned their heads quickly when he cast a glance their way. He uncorked the bottle and offered it to her with an apology. "No glasses, I'm afraid, Miss Willingham. Sorry."

She took his whiskey and sipped from the neck, making a face after she tasted it. "It's quite strong, isn't it?"

"You get used to it."

"I only drink whiskey for its medicinal qualities. I must admit my nerves are a little on edge over my teaching assignment in Laredo. I've been told Laredo is a very rowdy town." She put the bottle to her lips and drank again, a larger swallow.

"The city marshal is an old friend of mine. If you wish, I can make you acquainted with him, just in case you ever have need of the marshal's services."

"That would be very nice," Etta said, returning the bottle to him. She examined his face more closely in light from the oil lamps as the conductor left their car. "I'm curious as to your line of work, Mr. Slocum, and the fact that you feel the need to carry a gun."

He drank a generous swallow himself and sat back against his seat. "In recent years I've done some detective work for some of the railroads. Train robberies have been on the increase around the Denver area. I'm on my way to Laredo to help investigate the disappearance of a young woman. She was apparently abducted by a nefarious character who has taken her into Mexico. My friend, the city marshal, wired me to come down for a talk with him and possibly to find out where the girl might be. A fairly sizable reward has been offered for the girl's safe return, since those types of men are beyond the reach of Texas law south of the border.''

"There is no law in Mexico?"

He chuckled. "Not much, I'm afraid. The Mexican government is in a state of chaos right now. A revolution is brewing and it keeps them busy. I'll be acting on my own, unofficially, if I go down there to try to arrange for the girl's release."

"It sounds very dangerous. You must be a brave man to take that sort of chance."

Slocum grew more fascinated with Etta as time passed. She was indeed a beautiful woman. Emerald eyes watched him from a face made of flawless ivory skin. "I've never considered myself a particularly brave sort," he said. "Careful is a better word. I don't take big chances unless I calculate the risks beforehand. If I believe I can get the girl back to her sister unharmed, I'll make the attempt, but only when I'm convinced I stand a good chance of getting it done safely."

"It still sounds very courageous. Something could go wrong."

"I try to allow for that. Being prepared is the best remedy for most unexpected surprises." He drank again and offered her the pint.

Etta took the bottle and swallowed a more liberal amount this time. Outside the passenger car window, darkness settled over thorny brushland like a black blanket. She puckered some when the whiskey burned her throat. "In spite of the terrible taste I do feel more relaxed now," she told him. Her green eyes came to meet his. "Do you have a family, Mr. Slocum?"

He shook his head. "My father and brother were killed in the war. My mother died of grief afterward, or so I was told. She was dead before I could get home from Kansas. I was wounded in a fight with some Jayhawkers just as the war was coming to a close. I've never had a wife or children. I suppose I never found a woman who could tolerate my wandering ways. I get this urge to see the other side of a mountain sometimes. I've been on the move a lot since the war."

Etta's eyes sparkled in the lamplight. "Maybe you never found the right woman who understood you."

"I reckon that's a possibility. Not many women will abide long absences from a man." As he was thinking about the truth of what he said, he was listening to the distant chug of the engine. "Maybe the right woman just hasn't come along yet," he added with a grin. "I haven't given up looking."

She reached for the pint of whiskey and drank from it as the train rounded a curve. Slocum thought he noticed a hint of color in her cheeks.

"I have arranged for a room at a boardinghouse in Laredo," she said. "It's close to the school. Perhaps, if you have time and the inclination, you could pay me a social call there. It's called Grayson's, on Santa Maria Road."

He knew the whiskey was loosening her up now. "When we get to Laredo I'll be glad to escort you there in a rented carriage," he said, "Laredo can be a dangerous city late at night."

Etta's blush deepened. "Why, that would be quite gentlemanly of you, Mr. Slocum. I'll gladly pay for the carriage. I have some money, a small amount."

"That won't be necessary, Miss Willingham. I'd planned to rent a carriage to carry my own belongings to my hotel.

We can ask for directions to Grayson's as soon as we get to town.''

She gave him a very different look then. ''I must admit I was wrong about you, Mr. Slocum, believing you were something of a rogue. You are truly a gentleman who wouldn't take advantage of a woman traveling alone.''

He rested a booted foot across his knee. ''It never crossed my mind to take unfair advantage of a lady,'' he told her, noting that almost half the whiskey was gone.

Outside the car, sounds from the steaming locomotive echoed across a stretch of flat prairie. He judged they were still two hours from Laredo.

The sounds of the locomotive came through the windows as miles passed beneath the wheels.

She was decidedly drunk, unable to stand without assistance when he held her by the arm. He guided her up the stairs to his room at the Posada Hotel. She giggled every now and then, when she lost her balance on the steps. Escorting her down a darkened hallway with a young Mexican boy carrying her trunk and carpetbag, he hoped Etta wasn't too drunk to enjoy the rest of the evening. Unlocking his door, he instructed the boy where to put her belongings and paid him a quarter. As soon as the door was shut, he helped her to the edge of the bed and lit a lantern.

''It's hot in here,'' she gasped, unfastening the top button on her dress. ''Please open a window. Perhaps it's the whiskey making me feel hotter.''

He opened a window and took off his coat, then came to the bed and offered her the last swallow of whiskey. She took it and sighed.

''Let me help you out of your dress so you'll be cooler,'' he suggested, opening another button, and yet another.

''Please turn down the lantern,'' she whispered huskily, a faraway look in her eyes. ''I really shouldn't be doing this. It's so unladylike to undress in front of a strange man. We scarcely know each other at all."

He bent down and kissed her lightly on the lips. "We know each other well enough, Etta, and this room is so terribly hot."

She assented by nodding once while he continued to unfasten her buttons. He drew her gown over her milky shoulders and let it fall to her waist. Then he kissed her again, longer this time, and with more passion. A quiet moan came from her throat. She reached for a drawstring gathering her corset in front, and untied it. Her ample breasts strained to be free of the fabric, and as she opened the front where it was joined, her bosom mushroomed to a size even Slocum had not predicted. Her breasts were large, well formed, rising from her chest. Her nipples were small, pink, and twisted into hard little knots.

"Please turn down the lantern," she said again, trying to cover her naked breasts with small hands. "It isn't proper for a man to see a woman like this."

He reached for the wick and lowered its flame until the room was almost dark. Then he kissed her again and started taking off his shirt.

"Oh, John," Etta whispered when he drew his mouth away.

Gently, he laid her across the mattress and pulled her dress over her hips, leaving her wearing nothing but her stockings and high-button shoes. He removed his gunbelt, then his boots and pants. When he lay down beside her, he could hear her breathing hard and smell her perfume. Carefully, he put his arms around her and drew her body against his.

"I don't want you to think I'm some kind of trollop," she said softly. "I've never done this sort of thing with a total stranger. But you are so ruggedly handsome, and the whiskey has made me forget that I'm a schoolteacher. Please be gentle with me, John. I'm not very experienced. . . ."

He cupped one breast in his hand. Kissing her lightly on her neck, he whispered, "I promise I'll be gentle."

She crossed one shapely leg over his hips, bringing her soft mound close to his belly. Slocum ran a hand down her thigh to her knee, then up the curve of her leg to her buttocks.

"Oh, John!" Etta gasped when she felt his erection touch her abdomen.

He curled his fingers into the moist lips of her cunt and left them there, feeling her warmth. She began to breathe harder in short, rapid bursts. For now he'd forgotten all about a girl being held prisoner by Luis Zambrano and his bottles of laudanum. Tonight he was finding rapture in the arms of Etta Willingham, and business would have to wait until morning.

Later, he entered her, very slowly, carefully, so as not to hurt her. When his prick slid inside her, she shuddered and bit her lip to keep from crying out. An inch at a time, he pushed his shaft into her, until it felt as if there were no more room for him there.

Reflexively, Etta began to hunch against him, tentatively at first, groaning each time she thrust against the base of his thick member.

He matched every upward push of her groin with pressure of his own, feeling her muscles tighten, listening to her soft moans of pleasure. The bed began to rock. Outside his hotel window all was quiet in the streets of Laredo, for the hour was late, well past midnight. Very gradually the tempo of their lovemaking increased, and now metal bedsprings made a creaking sound with every movement they made. Etta's moans became louder, and to stifle them she gently bit the lobe of his right ear.

His balls exploded inside her a quarter hour later, after the woman's second climax. They fell asleep in each other's arms, and slept soundly until dawn.

8

Tom Spence looked much older than Slocum expected. Tom's face sported a gray handlebar mustache, and his sideburns were graying. Slocum didn't bother to count the years since they'd seen each other, nearly six by his rough guess. Entering the city marshal's office, he almost didn't recognize the man seated at a rolltop desk against one wall.

"Is that you, Tom?" he asked, closing the door behind him.

Tom's face broke into a wide grin. "It's me, all right. I would have known you anywhere, John Slocum. Wouldn't have needed to ask." He got up quickly and strode across the room to shake Slocum's hand. "Damn, Johnny boy, it's mighty good to see you. Been a long time since we had a handshake. Last time I remember was when you came down to rescue that Anderson girl, Melissa, from Victoriano Valdez. I was half scared I'd never set eyes on you again. It's a rotten dirty shame we ain't kept in touch with each other. Partly my fault, I reckon. Keepin' the peace in Laredo can be a full-time job."

"This ain't the quietest place I've ever been," Slocum agreed. "I was in Abilene when I met a pretty lady. She said she needed to have me come down and look for her sister.''

"Take a seat," Tom suggested, pointing to a leather-bound chair beside the desk, still grinning from ear to ear. "I've got coffee made. I'll pour you a cup an' we'll catch up on things."

Slocum took the chair Tom offered. "Not much to tell, Tom. I've been working for the railroads for a while. Handled a few other odd jobs, traveling around a bit, seeing places I've never seen, selling a few good horses. I've been making a living, I reckon."

Tom went over to a potbelly stove where a smoke-blackened coffeepot gave off mouthwatering smells. He took a tin cup off a peg near the stove and poured coffee. "I'm mighty glad you came, Johnny." He carried the cup over and handed it to Slocum. "So tell me what brings you down to the border again. Seems like it's always trouble."

"There's a girl. She was taken prisoner by one of the worst of the border outlaws, or so I'm told. A man by the name of Luis Zambrano. She was drugged while she was up in Abilene by a fella calling himself Smith. Smith was simply being paid to find a white woman for Zambrano and bring her to Mexico. I'm sure Smith has left this part of the country by now. He was a decoy."

Tom returned to his chair, giving the office wall a thoughtful stare. "I've notified the *federale comandante* in Nuevo Laredo, and informed the Texas Rangers," he said. "They know Zambrano, if nothin' else by reputation. Every no-account saddle tramp in this part of Texas asks me about Zambrano because of the rewards, but not one of 'em looks like a man who can get the job done. If there's a way to find her, I know you'll be the one to do it. But I can promise you it'll be tricky. Zambrano is a ruthless cutthroat, an' he ain't nobody to fool around with, Johnny. He's one of the meanest sons of bitches in northern Mexico. If he thinks you're on to him, he'll kill the girl an' likely make things rough for whoever gets too close to him.''

Slocum had been thinking while Tom was talking. ''Will he listen to an offer of ransom? If the girl's sister offered him a chunk of money for her safe return, would Zambrano listen?''

''Hard to say,'' Tom remarked, rubbing his chin. ''Money can do powerful things, but nobody knows Luis well enough to figure out how his mind works.''

Slocum considered it more thoroughly. ''How tough would it be to contact him without getting my head shot off?''

Tom shrugged. ''It'd only be a guess, but Luis might think it's a trick of some kind, figuring he'd be walkin' into a trap. If he suspicioned he was bein' set up, he'd be twice as dangerous.''

''If there was someone he trusted . . .''

''Men like Zambrano don't trust nobody.''

Slocum took a sip of coffee as an unexpected recollection of the time he'd spent with Etta Willingham entered his thoughts. She had been so embarrassed this morning when she awoke beside him at the hotel. Finding herself completely naked, she'd covered her body with a sheet and started to cry, blaming whiskey for her unabashed behavior. He'd been finally able to comfort her enough so she could get dressed without shedding more tears. On the drive out to her boardinghouse she'd begun crying again. He'd halted the rented carriage under a live-oak tree long enough to convince her that she'd done nothing wrong, that two people had met and shared a special evening together. He'd promised to call on her again as soon as his business in Laredo was finished, and that had seemed to console her somewhat.

''I met a beautiful lady on the train, Tom, a schoolteacher by the name of Etta Willingham. If she ever needs help,

I'd be obliged if you'd see what you can do for her."

Tom chuckled. "That part of your disposition ain't changed none over the years. You always was quite the ladies' man. Did you ever take a wife?"

Slocum shook his head. "Is Maria still with you?"

"I got married to Maria a few months after the war was over. You met her when you were here the last time. I've already told you the story. We met in a roadhouse close to Memphis. She's a Mexican girl an' Laredo was her home. That's how come I wound up here. Followed her back an' we got hitched. We've got four kids, nearly all of 'em grown up an' moved off. She ain't gonna leave me. Hell, I think she enjoys stayin' just so she can make me miserable, like when we were at Bull Run. Remember?"

"I'd just as soon not talk about the war. I've tried real hard to forget it."

Tom nodded his agreement. "Me too. There's some things we hadn't oughta remember. Good to know you feel the same way . . ."

Slocum drank more coffee. "I suppose the first thing is for me to find this Luis Zambrano. When can you arrange it?"

"I can't say for sure. I got word he was in Nuevo Laredo now, but his regular hangout is south, at Sabinas Hidalgo."

"See what you can do. If I decide to head into Mexico to look for this Zambrano, I'll need a horse that's wise to the desert. Maybe a spare horse, just in case I find the girl."

Tom stood up, wincing a little, as though his knees gave him pain. "I've got a good grulla gelding I'll loan you. Stout as a Missouri mule when it comes to packin' a load, and he can run. He was raised on a ranch west of here and he's bred for this type of dry country. Also got a sorrel that'll work." He chuckled. "Seems like I was loanin' you dry-country horses the last time you was here. Hell, that's what friends are for, Johnny."

Slocum got up, and that was when Tom noticed his gun.

"I see you carry a Peacemaker model. Damn reliable gun, but I never did cotton to drawin' across my belly like that."

"It took a little getting used to," Slocum agreed, following Tom out the office door while taking note of the pistol Tom carried, a .44-caliber Mason Colt conversion tied low on his right leg. "I see you prefer a Mason."

Tom locked the door behind them. "Damn near any side arm is better than them Dance pistols the Confederacy issued. Worst gun to misfire ever was made, unless you count them early Walkers. I got me a bellyful of misfires durin' the war. Made myself take an oath I'd never own another unreliable shootin' iron. In my profession a feller can't afford but one mistake. I wouldn't trade this Mason Colt for all the pistols in the world."

Slocum led the way to his carriage, and climbed in the front seat. Tom was a little slower with his bad knees.

"Head southwest along the river," Tom instructed, pointing with a gnarled finger that appeared to have been broken sometime in the past. "I'll take you to my place so you can say hello to my wife Maria. Then we'll get those horses from the corral."

Slocum wheeled the rented buggy horse and slapped reins over its back, driving off in a cloud of yellow caliche dust rising up between rows of small stores and shops. A few people were out and about on city streets, although it was early, before ten o'clock. He saw a side street lined with saloons and cantinas on their way out of town, remembering that district as the toughest part of Laredo. Tom Spence had one hell of a job to handle here, and the simple fact that he was still alive serving as a lawman on the Mexican border was proof enough that he knew how to take care of himself in a tight spot.

Leaving town down a rutted road running beside the Rio Grande, Slocum admired big cottonwoods along the river's edge and, here and there, drooping willows that grew on the banks. Grass was abundant, making the river an oasis passing through one of the worst stretches of desert in the entire Southeast. Water gave life to it. The Rio Grande was the only reason towns like Laredo and Del Rio and Eagle Pass could exist. But the river was much more than water; it was a magic boundary beyond which men wanted by the law couldn't be touched. Just south of the river, desperados of every description lived beyond the reach of warrants for their arrest from most every state in the Union. Slocum remembered the frustration he'd heard from Texas Rangers who had trailed their quarry hundreds of miles, only to be forced to give up and turn back on the banks of this river. If Slocum decided to cross it, he would have no legal authority whatsoever, and only by living by his wits could he hope to stay alive.

"Looks mighty peaceful, don't it?" Tom asked, sighting down the Rio Grande's lush banks. "What most men don't realize is that just over yonder lies a haven for every type of sorry son of a bitch on earth. A blindfolded man could throw a rock most any direction an' be damn sure of hittin' a wanted outlaw two out of three times."

Slocum chuckled softly over Tom's words, but in his heart he knew just how right Tom was. Crossing that river was akin to going to war.

9

A blistering midday sun turned the streets of Laredo into a furnace. Hot wind coming from the south stirred clouds of dust from caliche roads and patches of barren earth between buildings. Dust rose in swirls, whipped by gusts of wind, forming cyclones only a few feet high, whirling off into the surrounding brushland until they ended abruptly, their winds spent. Tom called them dust devils, cursing each time one swept past his porch as Slocum was packing his gear on the saddle Tom had loaned him. The grulla gelding stood almost sixteen hands at the withers, its hide covered with old ranch brands on its flanks and shoulders. Old scars on its legs evidenced hard use in rough terrain and a few mishaps with tangled lariat ropes. But the grulla was just the type of horse Slocum needed for a hard ride into the Tamaulipas desert, a range-bred mate for the sorrel Tom had also loaned him.

Slocum was dressed very differently now as he prepared for his journey toward Sabinas. He wore faded denims and a bib shirt, with stovepipe boots and spurs, abandoning his city attire for clothing more suitable to blast-furnace heat. He carried only a spare shirt and socks, and food in the form of jerky, tortillas, and coffee. His bedroll was tied behind the cantle, his war bag on a loop from the saddle-horn. Saddlebags held a wide assortment of personal amenities: a razor and soap, a shard of mirror, a few medicines. The rest of his equipment could be called armament: a Winchester Model 73 saddle gun in a boot below his right stirrup, a Greener twelve-gauge shotgun with barrels sawed off to twenty inches tucked inside his bedroll with its stock exposed. In his left boot a scabbard kept a bowie knife hidden. He wore his Colt Peacemaker, and carried the little Remington bellygun inside his shirt. The rest of the weight the grulla carried consisted of two canteens, a small sack of corn for his horses, and cartridges for each of his guns.

Tom inspected Slocum's preparations from the shade of his front porch without offering comment. His plump wife, Maria, was beside him. Their small house sat at the western edge of town in one of the poorer sections, proof that a city marshal's pay was a little short of what Tom might have wished for.

"That's about it," Slocum said, hanging his canteens from a pair of saddle strings below the front forks. Both horses stood hipshot in the oppressive heat, tails to the wind, heads lowered to keep dust from their eyes. "I reckon I'm as ready as I'll ever be."

Tom came to the edge of the porch. "There's a telegraph in Sabinas. Wire me if you can, or if you run into trouble. You know there ain't much I can do from here, but I'll do whatever I can."

Slocum offered his hand. "Thanks for everything, pardner. I'll send a wire if there's a need. Can't say how long I'll be gone, but I figure you'd already guessed that."

They shook. "Best of luck, John," Tom said, sounding a bit worried. "Wish the hell I could go with you. It'd be like the good old days, the two of us watchin' each other's ass."

Slocum thumbed back his hat to sleeve sweat from his

forehead. "The old days you're talking about weren't all that good, if you'll remember. Besides, I wouldn't ever want to go back to eating boiled acorns and being hungry all the time." He grinned. "Don't worry none about me, Tom. I'll be okay. I make it a practice never to ride into anything I can't get myself out of in a hurry."

A gust of wind blasted down the road in front of Tom's house as Slocum mounted his horse. Reining away from the porch, he touched the brim of his hat in a lazy salute and tickled the grulla's ribs with his spurs. Leading the sorrel, he rode for the river at a jog trot, tilting his hat into the wind to keep grit from his eyes. He rode back streets, keeping away from the business district so it was less likely anyone would see him when he left town. Tom had informed him that several bounty hunters had come to Laredo seeking the reward money being offered for Zambrano on both sides of the river, and that the hunt for Zambrano and Alice Drake might get crowded. Slocum wondered if one of the fortune-seekers was Cabe McAlister. McAlister stood about as much chance of finding Amanda's sister in this unforgiving land as he might looking for bullfrogs in a cactus patch.

Southwest of town Slocum found a shallow crossing, and sent his horses into the sluggish current. The Rio Grande was low in summer, hardly more than belly-deep on his animals in the deepest spots. Spread across the south bank of the river, the city of Nuevo Laredo, mile after mile of tumbledown shacks and shanties built of adobe, rested in a broad valley ending in a desert so vast and forbidding that only men who knew its secrets ventured across it. A winding road ran due south to Monterrey, passing through tiny villages where travelers could secure water and a few necessities, and occasionally decent food if a man knew where to look. Slocum had traveled this road a few times, although not in recent years, and he expected some changes.

Riding out on the south bank, he swung around the city on less-traveled paths seeking the main road to Monterrey, hoping to avoid any *federale* patrols that might ask questions. He carried papers of identity, but he preferred being allowed to inquire as to Zambrano's whereabouts at a particular cantina south of town.

He struck the main road half an hour later, after learning that Zambrano had headed south to Sabinas Hidalgo only yesterday, and slowed his horse to a walk, saving its strength from being sapped by heat. Traveling at night, he could spare his animals and himself a measurable amount of misery. Changing horses often would allow him to cover more country, and if he avoided riding during the worst heat of the day, both geldings would be in better shape by the time he got to Sabinas.

He remembered the village of Sabinas Hidalgo between Nuevo Laredo and Monterrey, and hoped he might make a few inquiries at a little *mercado* there, to see if anyone would tell him more about Zambrano, his habits, and his haunts. Sometimes a piece or two of silver elicited the information he couldn't get otherwise. Money was scarce in this part of Mexico, and a few silver coins spent in the right places might provide him with a scrap of news concerning Zambrano. If he were pressed for reasons, he meant to say he was considering the possibility of joining up with Zambrano, if the pay was right. He wouldn't be mistaken for a Texas lawman, since everyone knew American peace officers never came across the border looking for wanted men. The American treaty with Mexico prohibited that sort of thing outright, although sometimes a courageous bounty hunter slipped into the country hoping to make a payday.

Heat waves arose from the desert brush on all sides of the road, creating the illusion of distant lakes. Soon both horses were sweating, and a trickle of sweat had begun down Slocum's back that quickly plastered his shirt to his skin. Mopping his brow now and then with a shirtsleeve, he continued to push down a deserted roadway crossing empty land. An occasional adobe farmhouse sat off in the brush, but for now no one was about during the worst heat of the day to see him passing through. In the distance to the south and west, he could make out shapes of craggy mountains rising from the desert floor. The eastern edge of the Sierra Madres looked dim, far away. Suffering along with his animals, Slocum headed toward those far-off mountains at a slow pace, knowing that progress of any kind was better than none at all.

As the sun moved toward the west above him, the winds died down to a whisper. Listening to the clatter of shod hooves on sunbaked ground, he passed time thinking about other things. A time or two he was distracted by rattling from a bed of cactus or a clump of brush, when he rode too close. The grulla snorted and swung wide of the deadly sound, wise to the ways of rattlesnakes in this region where a misstep could mean twin fangs filled with poison. Here and there, horned lizards scurried away from his shadow. Again Slocum was reminded that damn near everything in this part of the world had thorns, fangs, or razor-sharp spikes.

One of the greatest hazards was a desert scorpion—its sting was sometimes fatal, for in some instances they grew to six inches in length and their venomous tails, under the best of circumstances, produced days of lingering fever and excruciating pain. Of less concern was the ponderous lizard called a Gila monster, with a bite so poisonous it left men bedridden for weeks. But most dangerous of all were creatures of the two-legged variety, men with guns and bad intentions who would rob and kill travelers for the weight of their purse or the horse they rode. South of the Rio Grande, a wise man expected the worst from every situation, and it was a pleasant surprise should things turn out otherwise.

Sunset brought a noticeable cooling to the desert. Purple shadows fell away from cactus, cholla, yucca, and tangles of mesquite. Spiny ocotillo plants offering no shade during the day cast curious images on the desert floor when the sun lowered. A rare tree of any size, most often an old mesquite gnarled and twisted by years of drought, sometimes appeared in the middle of a plain surrounded by clumps of brush. Mile after mile of flat sameness lay before him as dusk became dark. Although it would be cooler traveling at night, the hazards increased. Rattlesnakes fed at night, as did many other desert creatures. And in the dark, bandits often took advantage of the element of surprise when a lone traveler wasn't paying close attention to his surroundings.

Night birds whistled and chirped from dark branches in the maze of thorns blanketing the land, and always there was the clop of horseshoes beating out a rhythm accompanying his slow progress southward. Now and then he stood in his stirrups for a better look at what lay ahead, a dark thicket close to the road where an ambush might await him, or a shallow arroyo where someone could hide until he got in rifle range. The farther south he rode, the more uneasy he became.

A squat adobe building with a thatched roof sat next to the road, golden light from its paneless windows casting pale yellow squares on the adobe hardpan around it. Six raw-boned horses were tied to hitching posts at the front. They bore open-tree saddles typical of those ridden by Mexican *vaqueros*. A pair of burros harnessed to a two-wheeled cart stood behind the adobe. Slocum took note of the horses, and decided to ride past the cantina in hopes of avoiding any trouble with tequila-fueled cowboys. He counted the horses again, figuring the odds. At least six men were inside the little cantina, and someone was there who drove the burro cart. The six could be simple cowboys having a drink after a hard day in the saddle. Or they could be highwaymen on the lookout for easy pickings, a lone traveler they could rob. A drink of whiskey or tequila, even a gourd dipper of pulque or a lukewarm glass of green Mexican beer, would have seemed nice after a half day's ride through this miserable heat and dust.

But in order to cut the trail dust from his throat, Slocum would have to take a chance that the men inside were friendly. It wasn't his nature to let others crowd him away from things he wanted, but a young girl's life might be hanging in the balance and should any misfortune prevent him from meeting with Luis Zambrano to try to arrange for Alice Drake's release, the girl might suffer longer needlessly. Slocum meant to do it peacefully, if he were able, or by force if it proved necessary. Thus he made up his mind to ride past the cantina despite a powerful thirst for distilled spirits. He had whiskey in his saddlebags anyway.

As he was trotting his horses past the front of the building, two men wearing sombreros came to the doorway to stare at him. He touched his hat brim and continued on down the two-rut road without slowing his horse's gait. He noticed that neither of the *vaqueros* were wearing gunbelts.

"Probably just cowboys," he told himself quietly, glancing over his shoulder once, making sure no one meant to follow him.

The cantina fell away behind him until he could barely make out light from the windows. Reaching into one of his saddlebags, he took out a fresh pint of sour-mash whiskey and pulled its cork with his teeth. He drank deeply, sighing, enjoying the subtle burn of good spirits sliding down his throat. It required only a slight tug on his reins to slow the road-weary grulla to a walk, so as not to spill a precious drop of whiskey.

"That's better," he said aloud after taking another swallow of corn squeeze, as it was called when he was a boy back in his native Georgia. Calhoun County was known across the state for its home-brewed whiskey, some of the best anywhere. His father had been a publicly religious man who disclaimed having a liking for liquor, calling it the Devil's brew. But in private, William Slocum kept jars of whiskey hidden in the barn, and on more than one occasion John had found his father kneeling behind a haymow with a jar of Devil's mixture held to his lips.

Slocum drank again, and returned the cork to the neck of his pint, after a warm feeling began to spread from the pit of his stomach to other parts of his body. He was somewhat hungry now and at the next opportunity, when he found a piece of ground high enough to allow him to see in every direction, he meant to stop long enough to chew jerky and eat a couple of Maria's tortillas. His horses needed water and a handful of corn, yet finding water presented a problem of major proportions. There had been a water trough behind the cantina, but the risks of stopping had seemed to be too great. If he remembered the road correctly, Sabinas Hidalgo was only a few hours further south. There, he expected to be able to find water and fewer risks of any problems with roving bandits, unless he came face-to-face with Zambrano by accident.

As he was putting his whiskey back in his saddlebags, he took a look down his backtrail, and what he saw brought him up short, straightening in the saddle. A group of horsemen was following him—he could see their pale dust rising from the road even in light from a sprinkling of stars.

"Trouble headed my way," he muttered, reaching for his Winchester.

10

Slocum kept his horses in a steady lope toward the lip of a shallow ravine where the road made a bend, certain that the men behind him were from the cantina, and that they were bent on ill purpose. Sighting over his shoulder, he could make out the dim outlines of riders coming for him at a gallop. A gunfight was in the offing, a battle over his horses and saddles and what gold and silver he carried in his poke. Depending upon how well his pursuers were armed and how desperate they were, he could be in for the most one-sided fight of his life.

He reined over the top of the ravine and felt his horse make a plunge to the bottom. The arroyo was scarcely six feet deep, but it would be enough to provide cover from flying lead. As he swung down from the saddle, he fashioned a loop in one rein and tied it to a branch of a nearby mesquite bush before scrambling to the top of the cut-bank with his rifle. Levering a cartridge into the firing chamber, he peered over the rim just as six men spurred lathered horses toward the arroyo at full speed, manes and tails of their horses flying in the wind. He could hear the clank of spur rowels drumming against the horses' sides above the rumble of drumming hooves. With two hundred yards be-

tween him and the Mexicans, he rested his rifle sights on
one rider at the front, waiting, aiming high for the cone-
shaped crown of his sombrero.

"I'll warn him first," Slocum snarled, feeling the beat
of his heart quicken as danger came near. He curled his
finger on the trigger gently, a nudge that would not ruin
his aim.

His Winchester roared, slamming into his shoulder. A
ball of molten lead belched from the muzzle amid the clap
of exploding gunpowder. A stabbing finger of bright light
spat forth from the top of the ravine, and an instant later
there was a distant cry when a sombrero rose skyward,
spinning like a child's top above a rider's head. Riders
swerved off the road in confusion, trying to rein plunging,
frightened horses into the safety of the brush on either side
of the roadway. Shouts echoed through the night as men
called out to each other.

Two quick gunshots answered Slocum's rifle blast, the
pop of pistols. Somewhere high above Slocum's head, a
slug whistled away harmlessly toward the stars.

Performing mechanically, a practiced motion, Slocum
levered another shell into the firing chamber, paying no
heed to an empty brass cartridge casing tinkling musically
to the ground near his feet. Behind him, the grulla snorted
over the explosion and pawed the ground, although the
noise did not interfere with Slocum's concentration when
he sought another target among the dark shadows milling
about in the brushland. Riders charged in every direction
into the tangled thorns and cactus, hoping to escape the next
shot fired from the arroyo. One horseman toppled from his
saddle when his horse stumbled over something hidden in
the darkness—Slocum heard the man yell when he landed,
cursing in Spanish, apparently unharmed despite being un-
seated from a horse running at full speed before it fell.

"*Donde está?*" someone cried, asking where the rifleman was. Slocum spoke only a few words of Spanish, yet he understood the simple question readily enough.

The drum of hoofbeats faded, moving farther away.

"Maybe I scared 'em off," he whispered, scanning every foot of terrain before him, keeping his rifle to his shoulder.

A riderless horse wandered off, trotting back down the road in the direction from which it came. Hidden somewhere in a mass of thorny limbs was the Mexican who had fallen off. Slocum had to keep an eye out for a man afoot now, as well as watch for a return by the riders.

West of the road, three horsemen came together to talk over what to do next. One was hatless, the man who had ridden at the front when Slocum took aim at a sombrero. For a short time they sat their horses a quarter mile away, obviously discussing what had happened. Then one reined his mount for the wagon road and took off at a trot, heading back toward the cantina. A moment later the other two followed, casting wary looks at the ravine from time to time until they rode out of sight.

"Leaves three more," Slocum muttered. In the darkness and confusion he'd lost track of the men who'd scattered into brush on the east side of the roadway. Two were mounted, a third left on foot now that his horse wandered off. It was boiling down to a waiting game to see if the others rushed him.

Sweat trickled down his back and down his face from his hatband while he waited, watching closely for any sign of movement in the brush. His ears were still ringing from the rifle explosion so close to his face, and for that reason he couldn't quite trust his hearing. Cocking his head this way and that, he listened carefully for any strange sound, the slightest noise, as his gaze wandered back and forth across the dark landscape.

Then he saw them, two riders crossing a gentle swell in the prairie almost a mile away, backgrounded by night sky made bright by winking stars. The pair was leaving their horseless companion to fend for himself.

"Can't say your pardners turned out to be very good friends in a tight spot," he said quietly, addressing the unfortunate man who'd lost his saddle seat, though Slocum said it to himself in a soft voice only he could hear. But since he had no idea whether the Mexican was armed, it was a fool's move to ride out of the ravine until he knew the man's whereabouts. For the present it had become a stalemate of sorts, neither man willing to make the first attempt to withdraw from the scene or continue the fight.

I'll have to wait him out, Slocum thought, relaxing his grip on the stock of his rifle somewhat. Backing away from the rim, he walked quietly to his saddlebags and took out the pint bottle for a quick pull, to help steady his nerves. Even though the gunfight had been short, only three shots fired, it had been enough to rattle him a little.

Then he heard it, a distant wail in Spanish, a voice so thin he had trouble hearing it. *"Por favor, Señor!"*

Slocum hurried back to the edge of the cut-bank, peering over it cautiously. He saw a man standing a hundred yards away with arms raised over his head. Covering the Mexican with his rifle, he waited, puzzling over the voice.

"Por favor, Señor! Do not shoot me!"

Now the man spoke a mixture of Spanish and English. Both of his hands were empty. "Come over here!" Slocum shouted. "Keep those hands where I can see them!"

Slowly, one hesitant footstep at a time, the Mexican began to walk toward the arroyo with his palms held high. "Please do not shoot me, Señor!" he called again. "I have no gun!"

"Keep walking! I won't shoot so long as I can see that your hands are empty!"

Dodging thicker clumps of thorny plants, the Mexican continued forward, his spurs making a clanking sound when he struck a stretch of bare ground. Having heard the man's voice, Slocum realized he sounded young, hardly much more than a boy. The closer the man got, the more Slocum was convinced there was no harm in him now. He was skinny and short, slightly bowlegged, not threatening in appearance, and he seemed to be unarmed.

Slocum waited until the Mexican was ten yards away before he rose above the lip of the ravine to show himself, keeping his gun muzzle on the man's chest. "Keep coming," he said, motioning with his rifle barrel.

A boy walked up to Slocum, his face showing fear. He held his hands aloft, though they trembled greatly while he held them above his head.

"Why'd you and your pardners come after me like that?" he asked, lowering his Winchester when it was plain the boy wasn't concealing a gun.

The Mexican swallowed hard, "My *compadres* were very drunk, Señor. They wanted to take your money and your *caballos*. But when you shot off Arturo's sombrero, we were all very much afraid of you. My *caballo* fell in a gopher hole and I lost my *pistola* in the dark. Please do not kill me, Señor, for I am not a bad man in my heart. It was too much tequila that made us do this thing to you."

"I believe you. Tell me your name."

"I am Pedro Gonzalez. I am a *vaquero* for Rancho El Rio. I am not a bad man, I swear it before Dios! I drank too much of the tequila tonight and I listened to bad amigos who wanted to do a robbery. For this, Señor, I am very sorry. I pray you will not kill me for making this big mistake."

"I won't kill you, Pedro. You can put your hands down."

"Gracias, Señor," he said, lowering his arms to his sides.

Slocum wondered what to do with the boy. He had no

horse, and his friends had abandoned him as soon as the shooting began.

"How far do you have to walk to get to this ranch where you work?"

"Many hours, Señor. Rancho El Rio is near the village of Sabinas Hidalgo."

Hearing the boy's story, Slocum found himself feeling a bit sorry for the kid. "I'm headed that way. I reckon I could let you ride my spare horse most of the way, so long as you act real peaceable about it and don't try to run off."

"I would be very grateful, Señor. It is most kind of you to make such an offer to a bandit who was planning to rob you. I have only a little money, a few pesos, but I will gladly pay for the use of your spare horse."

"That won't be necessary. An apology will do . . . just make damn sure you don't have a gun hidden underneath your shirt. I'd hate like hell to have to kill you."

To show he had no weapon, Pedro pulled his homespun cotton shirt from his pants and turned around, revealing how thin he was under his clothing, bony ribs jutting through thin hide. "I have no gun, Señor. I owned an old *pistola,* but when my horse tripped I dropped it in the dark, and now I cannot find it. I give you my word I will not try to steal your horse, if only you will allow me to ride it to Sabinas."

"Come on over," Slocum said quietly, balancing his Winchester in his left palm. "You ain't much of a robber and neither are your amigos. They sure as hell ran off and left you the minute a slug got too close to 'em."

"It was the tequila," Pedro said again, walking hesitantly to the lip of the arroyo, grinning sheepishly. "We have never robbed anyone before. It was Arturo's idea, when he saw a lone gringo riding past Julio's cantina. Julio warned against it, but Arturo would not listen. I did not listen, Señor, and for this I am truly sorry."

"You've apologized enough," Slocum said, inclining his head toward the sorrel. "Mount up on that red gelding and we'll be on our way to Sabinas." It was then that a thought occurred to him. Perhaps the boy knew something about Luis Zambrano. "I'm on my way to Sabinas, trying to locate a bandit who's called Zambrano. I have a business proposition for him, if he'll listen."

Pedro stopped short, looking into Slocum's face. "You are seeking the dangerous *pistolero* Luis Zambrano?"

"That's him. I've got some money for him if he has what I'm looking for."

At that, Pedro stood a little straighter. "My cousin Raul Morales rides with Zambrano, Señor. I can take you to his camp, but I must warn you that it will be very dangerous. Zambrano has sworn to kill anyone who betrays his hiding place to the *federales*."

"I'm not a *federale*. I've got a business deal for Luis if he's interested in making some money. He took a girl with him from Abilene, and her sister wants her back badly enough to offer a five-thousand-dollar reward."

Pedro appeared to hesitate. "Maybeso I could ride there to tell my cousin about your offer. Raul can decide if Zambrano will listen to what you have to say."

"That'll be better than nothing, Pedro. You can make a few dollars in American silver by helping me out."

"How much silver, Señor?"

Slocum thought it over, considering the risks the boy would be taking. "Twenty dollars, after you take my message to Zambrano and get me an answer."

The boy grinned. "For twenty dollars I will take you to see El Diablo himself, Señor."

Walking over to the horses, Slocum booted his rifle and untied his reins. "Mount up," he said, sticking a boot toe in the left stirrup, pulling himself across the saddle. As soon as he was in the saddle he gave the boy the sorrel's lead rope. "Put a bridle on him and let's get started. Remember, I'm carrying a Colt .44, and if you try anything funny I'll put a bullet in you before you can get fifty feet away. The only way you'll live long enough to collect that twenty dollars is by doing exactly what you promised to do, take my message to Zambrano. Anything short of that will get you killed."

"I swear it, Señor. The only thing I ask is that we stop at the rancho to tell Señor Villareal I will be visiting my cousin. That way he will know where I am, and that I will return to work as soon as I have contacted Raul."

"Just so long as it ain't too far out of the way. The offer I have for Zambrano depends upon nothing happening to an American girl he has with him. If any harm has come to her, the deal's off."

Even in the dark Slocum could tell Pedro was frowning. "Why does Zambrano have this American girl with him, Señor?"

Slocum gave a measured reply. "Seems he may have taken her against her will by hiring someone to visit her in Abilene, then slowly feeding her bigger doses of laudanum until she was all but helpless. The gent wore fancy clothes, calling himself Carl Smith. Smith snuck her out of town while she was drugged and took her to Zambrano in Mexico. The girl's sister wants her back and she's more than willing to pay to get her out of Mexico. This is what I want you to tell your cousin, that I'm bringing a handsome offer for the girl's safe return to the border."

They rode out of the ravine at a walk, heading south.

"I will tell my cousin Raul everything," Pedro said. "You can be sure of it. I give you my word."

11

Alice stared out a window overlooking a walled courtyard, numbed almost to the point of unconsciousness. The bitter-tasting laudanum they gave her always made her so sleepy, and sometimes when Luis gave it too often, her arms and legs refused to work properly. It was when Luis came to see her that she was forced to drink the medicine. She had been told it was for the bleeding coming from inside her after Luis had had his way with her that first night. But the bleeding had stopped days ago, and yet she was still being forced to take swallows of the laudanum tonic, although it made her feel good a few minutes after she swallowed it.

Despite her sleepy condition, there were several things she was grateful for. Luis no longer required that she be tied to the bed when he used her, and when his prick entered her so deeply, it did not hurt as much as it used to. They also allowed her freedom within this upstairs room overlooking a courtyard and a pretty fountain. She knew they were in a village somewhere in Mexico—she remembered being tied to the back of a horse again and escorted by armed guards along a narrow trail to a walled city. The nights were cold and days were hot, like today. In pastures beyond the walled courtyard, she could see herds of goats grazing, being tended by small Mexican boys and dogs. The food they gave her was good, roasted quail or goat meat seasoned with chilis, sometimes a piece of beefsteak. And she'd noticed a subtle change in Luis lately. He was not as rough with her when he took her. Sometimes he could almost be gentle when his cock was inside her, unless he was drunk, which happened quite often.

She was given pretty dresses to wear made by women in the village, brightly colored gowns woven from spun cotton and wool dyed different shades with Indian designs on them. Every morning a Mexican woman brought buckets of steaming water to her room so she could bathe in a cast-iron tub behind a dressing screen in a corner of the room. The woman, whose name was Carmella, combed her hair for her and washed her clothes somewhere downstairs. A guard stood outside the door preventing Alice from leaving, but for the most part she was being treated well . . . until Luis came to her room. If only she had not begun a court-ship with Carl Smith when he came to Abilene . . .

Luis was a crude, insensitive brute who had no respect for her. The times he treated her gently were few, and even then he made her feel dirty, unclean, when he lay on top of her with his prick moving in and out of her. Sometimes he grinned at her with his horrible gold tooth gleaming in his mouth, and Alice could have sworn he was a likeness of the Devil, what scripture said the Devil looked like. All Luis needed were horns jutting from his head. There was a wickedness about him, a demeanor that was decidedly evil. His breath was always foul, and he was often dirty when he came to her room, reeking of sweat. He was the most repugnant man she could ever have imagined, and it was with him that she had first experienced what it was like to be entered by a man's cock.

Slowly, the sleepy feeling was ebbing away. Last night he had come to her room, forcing her to drink more med-

icine before he took off her clothes and pushed her down
on the bed. She no longer made any real effort to fend him
off, since it was useless to resist. He was much too powerful to deny him what he wanted, and when she had tried,
in the beginning, he'd hit her so hard that her face remained
swollen for days. Most of her bruises were healed by now,
but not the scars across her soul left by the dark knowledge
that he had taken away her virginity. She was a fallen
woman now, what some men called a soiled dove. No man
would ever want her, not after what Luis had done. Any
decent man would spurn her if he learned she was not a
virgin. A blacker thought was that she might not ever see
Texas again, or her sister, or the house in Abilene she loved
so much. It was quite possible that Luis would keep her
prisoner forever, or until he grew tired of her, and then he
might decide to kill her when he was finished using her.
At night she prayed that she would not get pregnant by him
and have his baby. It would be a fate worse than death to
bear a child fathered by such a horrible beast.

She knew her sister would be beside herself with worry
and grief. If there were any way to send help, she would
do so. But Alice knew that the laws in Texas were meaningless here, and that no lawmen from the United States
could enter Mexico to help her. Amanda would come herself if she could, if she knew how to handle this sort of
thing. But her sister was a peaceful woman and she wasn't
skilled with a gun. Someone would have to rescue Alice
who was a capable fighter, and judging by the number of
men Luis had with him, it would require a force of equal
strength to set her free.

Overwhelmed by so many dark thoughts, Alice continued to stare out her window sadly, wondering if she would
ever see her sister again, or Abilene. It had been the worst
day of her life when Carl Smith came to town and took her
away against her will, and she knew she would never forget

it as long as she lived. If only she had refused that first swallow of laudanum.

Watching the small fountain at the center of the courtyard, she let her mind wander, seeking more pleasant memories as if it might help shut out the horror of what had happened. . . .

Heavy boots sounded on the stairs. Alice recognized that sound, and she shuddered. Luis was coming for her. Steeling herself for what would take place, she sat on the edge of her bed and waited for the door to open. In spite of a wish not to, she felt tears forming in the corners of her eyes. She was too old to cry, she told herself.

Glancing out her bedroom window, she discovered it was dark. Somehow an entire day had passed without her realizing it. She knew it had to be the laudanum Luis gave her that was making her too drowsy to be aware of the passage of time.

A key entered the lock. Her door swung inward. Filling the door frame with his massive shoulders, Luis stood for a moment looking at her across the room, his gold tooth gleaming in light from the lamp on a bedside table. Alice saw the familiar lavender bottle in his hand.

"No more medicine, please!" she begged softly, as more tears came to her eyes.

Luis grunted. "It is not for you to decide, *mi hita.*" He came into the room slowly and closed the heavy oak door behind him. A guard's boots shuffled over in front of the door blocking anyone else from entering. Luis glanced down at the front of Alice's red cotton dress where it was open, revealing only the tops of her small, firm breasts. "Take it off," he snapped. "Then take a swallow of this laudanum. It will make you feel so much better. The doctor has promised it will make you well."

"But I'm not sick," she protested, "and it makes me feel so sleepy."

Luis's face twisted to a scowl. "Take it, *mi hita,* or I will pour it down your pretty throat." He came across the floor and took a cork from the neck of the bottle, glaring down at her with the blackest eyes she had ever seen.

She took the bottle and drank a small swallow.

"More," he insisted, the threat in his voice unmistakable in the silence of her room.

She drank again, making a face when its bitter taste made her pucker.

He took the bottle and corked it, placing it beside the lamp. "Now take off the dress, pretty one. Show me what your body looks like tonight. Every night I must be reminded of how perfect you are. Take the dress off slowly and drop it on the floor around your ankles."

She got up, feeling slightly dizzy the way she always did after taking laudanum, although sometimes the feeling was pleasant. Unfastening a cord binding the front of her gown, she let the ends fall loosely and wriggled her dress off her shoulders. She was naked underneath her gown and when Luis saw her pubic mound, the scowl left his face. He grinned.

"Turn around," he said huskily, eyes roaming up to the swell of her breasts, her hardening nipples. "I like to look at your ass, my brown-haired beauty. You have a nice ass, so soft and so round."

Alice turned, noticing that her dizziness had increased to the point that she feared she might fall. "The medicine," she said in a slightly fuzzy voice.

Suddenly her knees gave way. She fell across the bed on her chest, her mind swimming. A moment later she felt a hand cup one cheek of her buttocks. The mattress quivered when Luis put his tremendous weight on it. Alice felt him spread her legs as he came between them. Then the head of his cock touched her cunt and she winced.

He entered her, only the head of his thick prick stretching the lips of her cunt wide. A glimmer of pain flashed through her groin and she groaned in protest, "Don't hurt me, please . . ."

Luis laughed, a cruel laugh telling her how much he enjoyed hurting her this way.

"It will not hurt in a moment, *mi hita,* when your juices are making your pussy wet."

"It hurts," she said, the words slurred by laudanum and having her mouth pressed to the bedcovers.

He pushed more cock into her, another inch, grunting when he did so.

Alice closed her eyes, fighting back a rush of hot tears flooding her cheeks. She knew she could endure the pain, as she had so many times since they took her from Abilene. It was not only the pain bringing tears to her eyes, but the humiliation.

"Now it will feel good," Luis promised, as he began to make short thrusts into her cunt, driving his cock deeper.

But there was more pain each time he pushed his stiff prick further inside her, rocking the mattress with the power of his thrusts. Gritting her teeth, Alice dug her fingernails into the bedspread, preparing herself for more hurt. It was slightly more painful when he took her from behind, the way he was now, yet it did no good to protest this position.

The bed rocked and swayed as he drove farther up her cunt, until at last the hilt of his shaft was buried between the lips of her pussy. His prick throbbed with desire while his heavy hips drew his cock back and forth.

Soon she was gasping for air, panting, and as in the past on a few occasions, accompanying the hurt was a warm feeling that was part good, part pain. Zambrano's thrusts grew faster now as he neared a climax. With her eyelids tightly closed, she whispered to herself that soon it would be over.

He had been resting his weight on his elbows, when suddenly he fell across her back while hunching furiously to achieve his orgasm. His balls exploded and he let out a muffled yelp as his climax came.

Warm, wet seed spewed from his prick into her cunt and she gasped, barely able to breathe with his weight pressing her to the mattress. "Please get off!" she cried, the sound stifled by lack of air.

He thrust once more and grunted, sweat from his hairy chest wetting her back and shoulders.

"Please get off—you're too heavy!" she begged.

At last he lifted himself with his palms, his stale breath brushing her cheek when he said, "That was good, my pretty one."

Finally able to breathe again, she merely nodded, keeping her eyes tightly closed.

"Did you like it?" he asked, a hint of demand in the tone he used.

When she did not answer him immediately, he delivered a stinging blow with an open palm across her face. She cried out and drew away, watching him now to see if he meant to hit her again.

"Did you like it?" he shouted, filling the bedroom with the boom of his voice.

"Yes," she whimpered softly, humiliated and at the same time afraid he would strike her again if she refused to tell him what he wanted to hear.

He withdrew his softening cock from her and got off the bed to fasten the front of his pants. "Answer me the first time I ask you a question, *puta*!"

She could scarcely manage a nod with her mind afloat in the effects of laudanum, although she did so to keep from being hit. She felt his jism wetting the bed between her thighs as it went out of her, and she mouthed a silent prayer that there would be no baby forming inside her.

To stem another tide of tears, she thought about her sister, and about a favorite swimming hole in a creek along the northwest boundary of a friend's winter pasture where she swam in summer without her clothes. Sometimes she swam her chestnut pony into the creek so she could dive off its back. The swimming hole had been her own secret hideaway since she was old enough to ride there on her own. She only told her sister about it when Amanda asked why her hair was wet one summer day after she got home. It would be so nice, she thought, to be swimming in that deep pool of water today, rather than being held prisoner by a monster who used her so heartlessly in this way.

Her mind drifted away from those sweet recollections, and soon she was almost asleep.

The door closed gently behind her, and now the pain was less between her thighs.

12

Pedro rode beside Slocum across a prairie brightening with sunrise. The road to Sabinas Hidalgo ran arrow-straight through mile after mile of thorny undergrowth and scattered stands of mesquite trees. As dawn came, they passed occasional burro carts laden with woven baskets, clay pottery, and sometimes bushel bags of corn. Now and then a few *vaqueros* rode in small bunches toward another day's labor gathering wild longhorn cattle from land so impossibly dry and rugged that Slocum found it hard to believe animals could exist on it. From time to time they glimpsed a few longhorns moving through tangles of mesquite nibbling on beans growing from low branches. Mesquite beans were the only edible things in this wasteland, Slocum decided, besides a few clumps of dry bunchgrass hidden below a thorny limb or yucca spines.

Pedro talked freely now, apparently convinced Slocum wasn't going to kill him for his role in the attempted robbery. The boy told him several things about Luis Zambrano that might come in handy. Zambrano recruited men from mountain villages across Tamaulipas and Coahuila to raid cattle ranches in Mexico and Texas. Zambrano plundered rich ranches, sharing some of the spoils with poor people, making him something of a legend among simple *peones* who worked for wealthy landowners. Pedro's cousin, Raul, believed in Zambrano's raids because some of what was stolen was given to the poor. Of late, however, Raul had begun telling Pedro that he'd become disillusioned with Zambrano's promises. Zambrano continued to raid and loot ranches and larger farms for the booty, keeping most for himself. Men who rode with Zambrano were beginning to grumble that their leader did not believe in helping the poor after all, that he merely used it as an excuse for banditry. Slocum wondered how widespread this low morale was. Could it be a weak link that might allow him to get close to the girl?

Pedro pointed to an offshoot trail east of the road. "This is the way to Rancho El Rio, Señor. It is only a few miles to the rancho. I will tell Señor Villareal that I must visit my cousin for a short time. We can water these *caballos* there and be on our way *muy pronto*."

Slocum nodded, following the boy eastward when they came to a pair of dim ruts. Pedro didn't seem like a bad kid, but he occasionally listened to bad advice from his friends. During the night the boy had told him what it was like working on a cattle ranch in this unforgiving land. Water was as precious as gold to cowmen here and during a drought, cattle died by the score when wells dried up, or from starvation when there was no grass and a poor crop of mesquite beans. Life for a cowboy was equally tough when it did not rain. Men suffered along with animals when the corn crop came in short. Pedro recalled several years when there was hardly any food for his family. Being poor, going to bed hungry night after night, was one reason men listened to promises made by such as Luis Zambrano. Zambrano told them a new government was needed, to see that poor families got enough to eat, and if he could recruit more men, they would form an army and overthrow the government in Mexico City. The idea had broad appeal among men who were very hungry.

"How close is Zambrano's hideout to Sabinas?" Slocum asked.

"Not far," Pedro replied, a bit nervous about the question. "I cannot take you there, but I will go myself to visit Raul. I will inform Zambrano that you wish to see him about the matter concerning this girl, but I would be killed if I took you there."

"I understand. I was only wondering how far you'd have to ride to get there."

"Half a day's ride, Señor, into the hills. That is all I should tell you. Several times each year Zambrano moves to another village. *Por favor,* do not ask me to say any more."

Slocum let the subject drop. Half a day's ride in hilly country was probably only fifteen or twenty miles. Zambrano relied upon fear to keep his hiding place a secret. Shooting anyone who gave his location away was motivation enough to keep most wagging tongues still.

Crossing a gentle rise in the brushland, they came in sight of a ranch house and several pole corrals. The house was small compared to most, made of adobe mud, with a clay tile roof and a long porch across the front. The corrals held a few horses, a smaller number of burros, and a handful of thin longhorn cows in a corral by themselves.

"Rancho El Rio," Pedro said. "Do not worry. You will be welcome here."

They heeled the horses to a trot, angling toward a windmill and a water trough that sat beneath it. Both horses scented water, and the two riders had no trouble holding them at a steady pace. A black-and-white spotted dog began to bark at their approach from a shady spot on the porch. At the sound of the dog, a man came out of the adobe to shade his eyes from a rising sun to see who was coming.

Pedro turned in the saddle. "I would ask one small favor of you, Señor. Please do not tell Señor Villareal about what I did last night. Señor Villareal is an honest man and if he knew I was trying to rob someone, he would send me away."

"We'll keep it between the two of us," Slocum agreed, more than ever believing Pedro had been the victim of bad companions when he'd joined his friends for the robbery attempt.

They rode to the front of the house. An aging Mexican with a handlebar mustache nodded to Pedro, then to Slocum.

"*Buenas dias,*" the old man said, his gaze wandering to the guns Slocum carried.

Pedro jumped to the ground. "Señor Villareal, this is my friend Señor John Slocum. I must ask that you let me go to see my cousin, Raul, so that Señor Slocum might be able to do some business with him."

Villareal frowned looking at the boy. "Does this business have to do with Zambrano?" he asked sharply.

Slocum interrupted before Pedro could reply. "It has to do with money being offered for the return of an American girl who may be a prisoner of Zambrano. All I want to know is if the girl is with them. Pedro will not be involved. As soon as he has contacted his cousin he will be heading back here. There won't be any danger for the boy."

The old man listened, but he still seemed doubtful. "It is *muy malo,* very bad, for this boy to go there. Zambrano makes these young men bold promises, yet he does little to keep his word to them. I do not want Pedro to hear these false promises about great riches." He stared into Pedro's face. "Do not listen to Zambrano. From his lips only come terrible lies."

"*Sí,* Señor Villareal. I will not listen, I will only ask Raul

to inquire with Zambrano about a meeting with Señor John
Slocum. That is all.''

"Very well then, you may go. Come back quickly, for
there is much work to be done here.''

"May we water the horses?'' Pedro asked.

"Of course,'' Villareal said, pointing to the trough. "It
is common courtesy that any traveler may share what water
we have here. Let the horses drink, and fill your canteens.''

"I'm obliged,'' Slocum said, touching his hat brim. "I'll
be sure to have the boy headed back this way as soon as I
can. I aim to pay him for his trouble.''

When Villareal looked at Slocum's horses, his frown returned. He spoke to Pedro. "Where is the *bayo caballo*?''

Pedro blushed and looked at his feet. "The horse tripped
in a gopher hole last night. I fell off and the *bayo* ran away.
My amigo Diego will find it and keep it for me until I
return. It was a foolish thing, Señor Villareal.''

"Is the *caballo* injured?'' Villareal asked.

"No, Señor. It ran away like the wind. I walked to the
camp of Señor Slocum and he offered to let me ride this
sorrel to *el rancho*.''

The old man seemed satisfied. "Take another *caballo*
from the corral. You must have one to ride back from Sabinas when your business with Raul is finished. But remember what I told you about listening to Zambrano's
promises. He is nothing but a *bandido*.''

Pedro led the sorrel over to the water trough and handed
the reins to Slocum. "I will saddle another *caballo* and be
ready to ride *en un momentito, Señor*.''

Slocum swung down, weary after a night without sleep.
He let the horses drink their fill while he was filling one of
the canteens, noticing that Señor Villareal was talking to
Pedro at the corrals as the boy was saddling a dappled gray
mustang. It was easy to guess the old man was lecturing
Pedro about losing his bay horse last night.

Slocum passed a glance around the small ranch. It was spare and primitive in appearance, hardly the sort of cattle ranch one found north of the border. Life was hard for farmers and ranchers in this waterless part of Mexico. Livestock barely managed to exist on what little grazing there was. Cattle in the corral were mostly hide and bones and horns. He wondered how the old man showed a profit here from year to year.

Pedro came trotting from a small saddle shed leading his gray pony. By the color showing in his cheeks, he was smarting from the lecture Señor Villareal had given him. When he arrived at the water trough, he looked over his shoulder.

"Señor Villareal is very angry at me," he said. "He told me I should not have come back without the *bayo caballo*. I did not tell him the truth about how I fell. He warned me to come back in three days or I will not have a job at the *rancho*."

Slocum did not say that it didn't appear to be much of a job in the first place. He wondered idly what the boy was paid for wages. "Let's get moving," he said, mounting wearily, feeling sleepy. "If we push we can make Sabinas by late tonight, if we don't run into any trouble."

Pedro swung aboard his gray mustang and reined for the road to Sabinas, tugging his sombrero down over his eyes to keep out the sun. Slocum turned back and waved to Señor Villareal, who was watching them from the shade of a livestock shed. The old man returned his wave and went into the barn as they took off at an easy jog trot.

Turning south on the Sabinas road, they encountered more wagon traffic and travelers. Dust rose from wheels of big freight wagons drawn by oxen or spans of mules. Teamsters' whips cracked above the backs of laboring animals. Above the road a clear sky warned of another hot day as the sun climbed. They held their horses in a trot for half an hour, then slowed to a walk when heat brought sweat to the horses' coats. In places the road had turned to chalky powder where wagon wheels ground caliche to dust. Choking clouds of alkali hovered above the wagons and carts as they crept in both directions along what had become a very heavily traveled roadway. Slocum remembered Sabinas as being a small village on the road to Mexico City, which explained the much heavier wagon traffic heading to and from the town. Last night they'd had the road pretty much to themselves.

An hour later they rode through Aguas Calientes, hardly more than a water stop for thirsty teams and saddle horses crossing the Tamaulipas desert. A few dusty stores and shops advertised their wares with faded signs above windows and doors.

"If there's a good place to eat here we'll stop for a bite," Slocum suggested.

Pedro pointed to a tiny adobe building at the south edge of town. "Manuel sells the best *cabrito* in all the world, Señor. It is very spicy and we will need plenty of water, but the goat meat is good."

Slocum swung his horse over to a rail in front of Manuel's and got down. He handed Pedro a few pieces of silver. "Buy us a handful of meat and some tortillas. We'll eat in the shade of that big tree yonder. It's close to the well, so we can cool off our throats."

Pedro laughed. "A Mexican will not need water, Señor, but I think it would be wise for a gringo to fill Manuel's bucket, if you are not used to chilis and serranos."

The boy ran inside, sensing that Slocum wanted to avoid any unnecessary delay. While Pedro was buying goat meat, Slocum led their animals over to a towering live-oak tree providing shade over the stone-and-mortar lip around a well. He sent down a wood bucket on a piece of sisal rope, wondering how much longer he could go without a few hours of sleep. Already this difficult journey into the desert was telling on him.

Pedro hurried over with a piece of butcher paper wrapped around slices of delicious-smelling *cabrito*. Warm flour tortillas rested on top of the pile.

Slocum took a tortilla, noticing a thick layer of red pepper on each strip of meat, hoping he wouldn't regret having eaten a variety of food his stomach was not accustomed to. But when he bit into a sandwich of tortilla and *cabrito,* he was rewarded with a taste far better than he imagined. "It's mighty good," he told the boy, chewing contentedly.

It was half a minute later before the red pepper did its work on Slocum's tongue and mouth, sending him quickly to the bucket for a dipper of cool water. "That's hot enough to melt down a horseshoe," he said after several swallows.

Pedro laughed heartily, still eating without having taken a drink. "In Mexico you must like peppers," he said, grinning with a mouthful of food in his cheeks. "Otherwise, Señor, you will starve to death here."

They ate quickly and climbed back in their saddles. Slocum wanted to arrive in Sabinas before midnight, before he fell off his horse sound asleep.

13

Sabinas had a few large churches with tall bell towers, and old haciendas with walled courtyards. Tonight the town was quiet when Slocum and Pedro rode in. A number of lamplit cantinas sounded of guitar music and laughter, but most windows were dark. An adobe hotel sat across from a big central plaza, and seemed to offer spacious rooms. Slocum chose this place to spend the night. He was bone-tired and stiff from too many hours in a saddle. When he got down off the grulla gelding's back, he bent his aching legs to make sure they would support his weight.

"See if you can find a livery for these horses," he told the boy, taking down his bedroll and the rest of his gear, including his rifle. "I'll hire us a room. Make sure our animals get the best care, grain and hay. Don't worry about how much it costs."

He gave Pedro a few silver coins, and hoisted his war bag and guns for a slow climb up a set of stone steps to the front door. As Pedro was leading their horses away, Slocum stepped inside the hotel, too weary to think of anything beyond a clean bed and a few hours of badly needed sleep.

• • •

They ate a breakfast of chorizo sausages and eggs with warm tortillas before the sun appeared over the hills. They took their meal at a tiny street-corner cafe across the plaza from the hotel. Slocum felt truly rested for the first time in days. The people of Sabinas were out early herding goats down narrow roadways toward slopes thick with grass, buying food at a market west of the plaza, some driving burro carts loaded with all manner of wares.

A pair of mounted *federales* trotted their horses past the plaza.

"Where do you reckon those soldiers are headed?" Slocum asked, wondering if Pedro knew anything about *federale* patrols in the region.

The boy's cheeks were stuffed with food. He swallowed and pointed south. "They will ride the main roads, Señor. It is a show for the sake of the people, pretending to be soldiers. They see nothing and hear nothing. They do not look for a fight with anyone. *Los federales* are paid very little money. They have no heart for being soldiers because they are so poor."

"It don't appear anybody has any money down here," Slocum observed, casting a look around at signs of poverty everywhere his glance fell.

"This is the reason so many poor people listen to Zambrano," Pedro said. "He promises them he will give them money and land that once belonged to their ancestors if they join his gang. Raul says they are only empty promises. Señor Villareal has always told me the same thing, that Zambrano is nothing but a *bandido* who is telling the people lies."

Slocum thought about Pedro's attempt to carry his offer to Zambrano. "Tell Zambrano I'll meet with him at any place of his choosing, so long as I've got some assurances he is coming to talk terms for the girl's release. Tell him I'm offering five thousand in gold for her safe return."

Pedro nodded, wiping his plate clean with a tortilla. "I will return late this afternoon if all goes well. I must talk to Raul first, and then he will speak with Zambrano. If Zambrano wishes to arrange a meeting, he will send someone back with me who will talk with you personally, to see if you are telling the truth. Raul says Zambrano is a very suspicious man. He will make sure *los federales* have not followed me to his hiding place before he listens to what I have to say."

"Be real careful you're not followed by any soldiers," Slocum warned. He signaled for their waiter, and handed over silver when Pedro told him the price of their meal in American money.

They left the little cafe for a stroll down to the livery. As they were walking, Slocum thought about the risks facing the boy. He would have it on his conscience if Zambrano did anything to Pedro. He'd grown to like the kid more and more as they got to know each other.

At the musty stable a few blocks from the hotel, Pedro saddled his gray pony. Slocum kept an eye on the street until the boy was ready to leave. There had been no sign of *federale* patrols in Sabinas since he'd seen the pair at the plaza. Perhaps the boy was right, that these soldiers were merely putting on a show for the citizens, making them feel safe.

Pedro mounted and leaned down from his saddle. "I will be back before it is dark, Señor. If someone is with me it will be one of Zambrano's men, so do not be alarmed. I will come straight to the hotel."

Slocum thumbed back his hat so he could see the boy's face. "Don't turn your back on anybody up there, son. And be sure you tell them I'm not a lawman. I'm only here to pay money for the girl's safe return. Make damn sure you tell 'em that part, so nobody will think I'm a bounty hunter or a peace officer."

Pedro trotted his pony out of the livery, turning west. It had been Slocum's idea all along to see which general direction the boy rode.

Slocum walked back toward the plaza, idly listening to Spanish being spoken all around him. Glancing over his shoulder now and then, he made his way across the plaza to a narrow side street running up a steep hill. From there he would have a view of the countryside in every direction. The little gray mustang would be easy to see, even from a distance.

He watched the boy ride out of sight.

Facing a long day with nothing much to do, Slocum decided to locate the telegraph office Tom had told him about, take a hot bath, then find a quiet cantina where he could pass the hours sipping tequila.

Sauntering casually down to the plaza so as not to appear to be anything more than a sightseeing visitor, he turned north when he saw a row of telegraph poles coming down the side of a distant mountain. The poles ran to a small adobe building at the north edge of town. Passing time, he walked up a hill to the front of the telegraph office, peering through a window as he went past. An elderly man in shirt-sleeves sat at a desk where a telegraph key and a hand-crank generator rested in front of him.

"That's all I needed to know," Slocum said quietly as he walked around a corner of the building. "Only thing is, I sure hope that old man speaks some English."

He returned to the hotel, and spent almost an hour in a cast-iron tub in a bathhouse occupying a room off the back. A dark woman with Indian features carried pails of steaming water to him and later, clean towels. When he was shaved and dressed in his clean shirt, he strolled down to a street corner where an inviting little drinking parlor struck his fancy.

He went inside, took a seat at a corner table, and ordered

a bottle of tequila and a bowl of sliced limes.

Slocum drank slowly, chewing salted limes, watching the townspeople move about. He saw no more *federales,* and nothing else to indicate trouble might be lurking close to Sabinas.

A few hours later he went to the livery and saddled the red sorrel Tom had loaned him. The sorrel seemed to be the fresher of his mounts, and he cinched his saddle tight, ignoring the curious looks an old liveryman gave him as he paid his board bill for another night. It was doubtful Sabinas received many American travelers since it offered little in the way of accommodations.

Mounting up outside the stable, Slocum chose to ride in a southerly direction to see the lay of the land where Pedro had ridden. If negotiations with Zambrano went sour, it could be helpful to know where a few backtrails led, just in case he needed to make a hurried exit with bullets flying over his head.

He rode through the city at a walk, admiring old buildings as any stranger might. Several people gave him lingering stares when he rode past. At the outskirts of town he took a road due south, taking note of every offshoot trail heading into the hills and valleys. On many of the higher slopes he saw herds of goats and sheep, and a few cattle, most of the milking variety. He passed a few horsemen and an occasional donkey cart heading into town, but for the most part the road was empty.

Where the road climbed the side of a hill, he passed one of the more elegant older homes around Sabinas made of cut rock and mortar with archways for windows. A stone carver had cut a number of floral designs around doorways and window openings. It was an impressive house, larger than any he'd seen. A woman was outside tending to flower gardens. She watched Slocum ride by with a hint of suspicion, as if she knew he didn't belong there.

As he was cresting the top of a ridge running up the side of a mountain where the road dropped sharply into a narrow ravine, he almost ran headlong into a column of soldiers. A *federale* patrol was entering this same ravine from the south, and when he saw them he wheeled his sorrel off the skyline as quickly as he could. A narrow goat trail ran east into a line of pinyon pines, and he urged his horse to a gallop, hoping to make those trees before the *federales* reached the top of the ridge. Asking the horse for all its speed, he drummed his heels into the gelding's ribs until pine limbs brushed his face and arms. Winding along a switchback, the trail plunged into a rocky gorge where it continued eastward.

He reined the horse to a halt. "That's the last thing I need," he muttered, turning back toward town. He hoped to avoid being noticed by Mexican soldiers while he was there, just in case they started asking too many questions.

It was dusky dark by the time Pedro returned on his lathered pony. He found Slocum standing in the doorway of the cantina.

"Zambrano has moved to another hiding place," the boy, said after he jumped to the ground. "He and his gang have ridden east to Guerrero."

"Did anyone know if the girl is still alive?" Slocum asked softly.

"Yes, she is alive. I talked to an old *vaquero*. He saw them ride away from the hacienda where Zambrano had been staying for a few days. One of the women who works at the hacienda told me they were leaving for Guerrero, and that the girl is with them. They give her some kind of medicine and it makes her very sleepy. They put her in a cart and took her with them."

"How many men are with Zambrano now?"

"Only four. Many have deserted him because of his empty promises, but the four are very dangerous *pistoleros,* including my cousin, Raul."

"Makes five, including Zambrano."

"*Sí, Señor.*"

"Get something to eat. Tonight, we're riding for Guerrero, wherever the hell that is. . . ."

14

At the livery he saddled the grulla for himself and the sorrel for Pedro, giving the boy's winded gray a rest. The livery-man paid some notice to his gun and holster, although not in apparent alarm. Slocum and Pedro rode through the plaza under dark skies. Slocum was thinking how good a few shots of whiskey would taste. Pedestrians he passed along the road paid little attention to them, even though his dress and general appearance were very different from theirs. As far as he knew he was the only American in Sabinas at the moment, and this fact had begun to worry him a little. Word that a foreigner was in town might reach Zambrano, or the *comandante* of the *federales*. Would the *federales* be interested enough to question him about his reasons for being there?

As Slocum was dismounting, Pedro said, "I tell the *vaquero* there is *un norteamericano* who wishes to talk to Luis Zambrano about offering money for the return of the *norteamericana* girl."

"What did the *vaquero* say?"

"He say maybeso he know someone who tell this to Zambrano *muy pronto,* so you can talk with him."

Slocum wondered if giving the old *vaquero* such a message was a good idea. But unless he talked to Zambrano, there was no way to arrange for Alice Drake's release . . . if it could be done at all. "Stay with the horses. I'll be right back with my gear."

He entered his hotel by a side door to pick up his war bag and the rest of his belongings, a precaution in case the *federales* already knew of his presence and were watching the front for him to return to his room. But he found the hotel lobby empty and made for the stairs, taking them two at a time. Walking softly down a poorly lit hallway, he fumbled for his key and unlocked the door. Just as he stepped inside his room, he saw a blur of rapid movement to his right.

Something crashed into his skull, sending him spinning to the floor. He clawed for his gun, his vision clouded by winking lights from the blow to his head. Whirling over on his side, he aimed his Peacemaker toward a shadowy shape towering over him and quickly tightened his finger on the trigger.

A boot struck his gun hand, knocking the Colt from his grasp before he could get off a shot. His gun went clattering into a corner of the room, but not before Slocum crawfished backward as fast as he could, reaching into his shirt for the .32 bellygun. In a flash he had his smaller gun cocked and ready to fire, and the sound of a cocking pistol stopped the figure looming above him from coming any closer.

"I'll kill you!" Slocum swore, his head still reeling from being struck. "One step closer and I'll make a hole through your belly." He inched further backward, trying to clear his brain and his vision quickly enough to get off a perfectly aimed shot. A swarthy Mexican crouched a few feet away, most of his face obscured by the wide brim of a drooping felt sombrero. A pair of crisscrossed bandoliers heavy with brass cartridges adorned his chest. He held a pistol in his right fist with its muzzle aimed down at Slocum.

"I shoot you first," the Mexican snarled.

Slocum knew he couldn't back down. "Maybe. But I'll get off at least one shot, and a belly wound is a hell of a slow way to die. I don't know who you are and don't give a damn. I swear I'll kill you unless you lower that pistol and start explaining what you're doing in my room. And why you tried to burst open my skull like that . . ."

For a fleeting moment the heavy Mexican remained frozen in a crouch, gun covering Slocum. Then he slowly lowered the muzzle of his weapon. "I am from Luis Zambrano. You sent a boy to look for a gringo woman with brown hair. He say you will pay in gold for this woman. Luis will hear what you have to offer, but only if you come unarmed. Unless you give me your weapons, you will not be allowed to talk to Luis."

Still keeping a close eye on the Mexican's gun, Slocum felt a knot on the back of his head, touching it gingerly with the tip of a finger on his free hand. "I'm not so sure I want to go someplace I've never been without my guns. This could be a trick, so you can rob me. I'll warn you now that I'm not carrying money to be offered for the girl's release. I'm supposed to wire a friend in Laredo as soon as the deal can be arranged. Someone will have to bring the girl closer to the border, so there won't be any chance of a double cross on either side. You show me the girl and I'll hand over the money, if we can agree upon a price."

"Luis will not come near the border."

"He came once, when Carl Smith brought her to Laredo while she was drugged with laudanum. The girl's sister wants her back. All she wants is that girl safe on the north side of the Rio Grande. Let me talk to Zambrano. We'll arrange something."

Again, the big Mexican stated flatly, "Luis will not come to the border. Some other arrangement must be made if you wish to see the woman alive."

Very slowly, Slocum sat up from resting on an elbow. "We can talk about that, I reckon. But I'm not going any-place where I'm unarmed until I'm sure this isn't a trick. I told you before I'm not carrying any money, just a letter from a bank in Laredo stating that the money is there, ready to be paid if I give the word a deal has been made." He remembered Pedro, wondering if the boy was okay. "Where is the boy who was waiting for me with our horses?"

"He has been taken to Guerrero by his cousin. Luis will not come to Sabinas for obvious reasons. The *federale* gar-rison is here, and we are wanted by the *federales*. You must come with me, but only if you surrender all of your weap-ons. I took the rifle and shotgun you had hidden under your bed. You must give me the little *pistola,* and the gun I kicked from your hand."

It appeared the only way to talk business with Zambrano was on the man's own terms, yet the risks were tremendous. If Zambrano wanted, he could have Slocum executed if negotiations went poorly for the girl's ransom. It was grim news to learn that his Winchester and shotgun had already been seized. Armed with only a pair of handguns, he was all but defenseless should things turn into an armed con-frontation.

The Mexican spoke in a hoarse whisper. "If I meant to kill you, Señor, you would be dead now. When you came into the room I could have killed you easily."

What the man said was true. If Zambrano planned an ambush for him, it would have been all too easy for the Mexican to shoot him, the moment he carelessly opened his door. "I suppose that part of what you say makes sense. I walked in here without thinking. I got this bump on my head instead of a bullet."

A look of satisfaction crossed the Mexican's face for only an instant. "So you see, I am not here to kill you,

Señor. I am only to take you to see Luis. But there can be no guns if you wish to talk about the woman. If you are as you say, here to make an offer of gold for the woman, then there is no need for a gun.''

A thousand thoughts raced through Slocum's mind at once. It went against his grain to face any situation without a means of defending himself, yet it appeared this was the only way he could meet with the bandit who held Alice prisoner. It was a risk he ordinarily wasn't willing to take. But he decided he would be forced to live by his wits until he was in a position to set conditions.

"I suppose this doesn't leave me with much of a choice in the matter," he said, relaxing his grip on the .32. "If this is the only way, then it's pretty cut and dried. Either I give you my guns or there'll be no discussion about paying ransom for the girl."

"This is the only way, Señor. Give me the little *pistola* so we can be on our way to see the Luis."

Slocum took a deep breath and let it out slowly, in resignation. He'd come this far trying to arrange the girl's release. A pair of pistols wouldn't save his life anyway in a shootout with a gang of bandits. If he traded bullets with Zambrano's emissary now, the best he could hope for was a lucky shot through a vital organ, then a fast escape out of Sabinas ahead of the *federales* after shots were ahead at the hotel. "It seems you're holding all the aces. Here's my gun," he said, lowering the hammer on his .32 with his thumb, offering it flat on his palm.

The Mexican took his pistol, walking over to the wall where his Colt .44 lay. When both guns were stuffed into his belt, he nodded to Slocum. "Now we can go," he said.

Slocum picked up his hat before he climbed unsteadily to his feet, his head still reeling from the blow. Placing his Stetson gently atop his skull to avoid the swelling, he motioned to his saddlebags piled in a corner of the room. "I could use a drink of whiskey after getting my head smashed. There's a bottle in my gear over yonder . . . no gun, just whiskey.''

The Mexican inclined his head. He still held his pistol at his side, proving he didn't entirely trust Slocum. ''Bring the whiskey,'' he said, ''and this letter telling about the money in Laredo.''

He clumped over to his saddlebags and fished out the pint, then an envelope from the Laredo State Bank. Folding the letter into a shirt pocket, he pulled the cork and took a thirsty swig of sour mash. A dull pain radiated from the knot on his head to the base of his neck. Another pull from the bottle helped take his mind off a throbbing skull for the moment. ''That's better, only my head hurts like hell. Wish you hadn't hit me quite so damn hard . . .''

From the corner of his eye Slocum saw the Mexican holster his pistol.

''My orders were to take your guns or your life, Señor. A bump on the head is far better than a bullet hole. I am called Chico. When we go down the stairs, remember I will be behind you. Do not be so foolish as to try to run away. I will kill you if you try to run. Those are my orders.''

Slocum put the pint his pants pocket. ''You speak good English, Chico. I understand what'll happen if I try anything. I'm only interested in arranging for the girl's release. Nothing else matters to me.''

Chico motioned to the door. ''Someone will meet us at the bottom of the stairs. It is time to go.''

Slocum walked out into the hallway first, feeling naked without a gun. ''I'll lock the door,'' he said, putting his key to the lock as soon as Chico came out.

''Take the back stairs,'' Chico commanded, keeping his voice low. ''Walk down the alley and say nothing to anyone we meet on the way to the corner. I will be right behind you. A bullet so close will break your spine, Señor.''

Slocum went to the end of the hallway as quietly as he knew how, to a door opening above a set of steps leading down to an alleyway heaped with garbage. Stray dogs nosed through piles of refuse as the two men descended the stairway. The odor of decay filled their nostrils when they reached the bottom step.

"That way," Chico said, pointing west.

Stepping wide of garbage heaps, Slocum started down the alley holding his breath from the stench. He could hear Chico's heavy boots close behind him. They came to a side street, and Slocum turned south to where where his grulla was standing beside a pinto.

A few bystanders gave them curious stares as they walked to the horses. Some seemed to recognize Chico, even in the dark. Whispered words were spoken by a few when they saw Chico, yet no one gave him a sign of recognition, a wave, or a friendly smile. Slocum could only guess they knew him and feared him as an associate of Luis Zambrano.

At the corner, a tall Mexican who carried two pistols at his waist sat quietly on a chestnut gelding. Slocum didn't like the man's appearance at all—he had close-set, nervous black eyes and a perpetual scowl on his face. He figured to be the more dangerous of the two, judging by the look of him, the way he carried himself, and his habit of continually watching his surroundings.

He handed Slocum the reins to his grulla, then spoke to Chico.

"*Vamos. Ándale!*"

"*Sí, Juanito,*" Chico said, mounting the pinto gelding with a great deal of effort.

Juanito swung his chestnut around. He led the way down a dark side street away from the plaza.

Slocum found himself flanked by the two Mexicans, believing he was headed toward one of the most dangerous encounters of his life since the war. Worst of all, he was unarmed, except for the bowie knife hidden in his boot. A knife wouldn't be much help, he knew, surrounded by scores of Mexican bandits carrying guns.

15

They rode side streets, pausing at every street corner, and he knew Chico and Juanito were watching for *federales*. Slocum took every opportunity to size up his escorts when their attention was elsewhere. A sideways glance at Juanito further convinced him he was the most dangerous. Juanito carried a modified Walker Colt in a cutaway holster tied low on his leg, a rig designed for speed at the draw. Chico was a bullish man who would be awkward with a fast pull. However, Slocum needed no reminder of how well Chico wielded a pistol for a club. The knot on Slocum's head throbbed with each movement of his grulla as they trotted down back roads out of Sabinas. But given a choice of adversaries, he would much prefer to battle Chico with almost any weapon, including fists, for the big Mexican's movements were slow, just slow enough to give Slocum an edge. And besides, he owed Chico for that blow to his skull, which added a bit of anger and revenge to a choice between fighting one or the other. Under any other circumstances, he wouldn't let a thing like that pass without getting even.

Near the edge of town, as they were riding through one of the poorest sections where tiny adobe shacks were crowded together on narrow dirt lanes, he discovered that his shotgun and Winchester were being carried in a canvas sling on the off side of Juanito's horse. Chico had searched his room while he was riding south of town, confiscating his weapons and probably anything else of value in his saddlebags, including his boxes of ammunition. An afternoon's ride had cost him precious time away from the hotel and his weapons. Silently he cursed his stupidity for leaving town. He'd come to Sabinas on business, and had permitted a leisurely ride to get in the way.

But the forthcoming meeting with Luis Zambrano could be his his last business trip. He'd allowed himself to be disarmed by the men who were taking him to Guerrero. Never before could he recall heading into what he knew would be a potentially deadly situation without any way to defend himself.

They rode out of town into a forest of stunted mesquites, where Chico swung his pinto horse east. Chico now rode out in front, with Juanito bringing up the rear, sandwiching Slocum between them. As soon as they had ridden barely a quarter mile, they came to a rutted wagon road, and as Slocum predicted, they turned southeast.

Chico urged his horse to a lope, and Slocum hurried his own gelding to stay close. One part of a possible plan Slocum might have employed to get the girl out of Mexico was worthless now, he knew. If somehow he could have gotten her away from Zambrano by force or stealth and made a run for the border on better horses, he stood a chance of being able to outdistance men riding lesser animals. But now he was unarmed, making such a plan too dangerous. The only hope of bringing the girl back to Texas was to pay whatever ransom money Zambrano demanded for her, up to five thousand dollars in gold. Even then, the bandit might double-cross him at the last minute—nothing could be counted on until Alice Drake was safely across the Rio Grande.

The road twisted through mesquite-choked hills, then down into ravines, and then back to more hilly ridges. An hour away from Sabinas, they swung due east again and headed into a deep arroyo.

They rode to the bottom of the ravine and out the far side at a gallop, until the road climbed more steeply, forcing their horses to labor for air. Chico slowed to a trot, and so did the other animals. Once, Slocum glanced over his shoulder. Juanito stared back at him with hard black eyes made of pitch. Slocum had no doubts that Juanito would enjoying killing him should the need arise.

"I won't give him any excuse," Slocum whispered under his breath. "Not until I'm ready to make my move . . . if and when the time comes."

The road crested a switchback, where it plunged down a drop so steep their horses had to scramble for footing in spots worn down to loose rock. Slocum's head ached, and when he remembered crashing to the floor of his hotel room, he ground his teeth together in anger. There were times when he prided himself on how well he controlled his temper, yet there were also times like these when he battled urges to forget everything else and settle things with Chico.

The trouble was, the only weapon he possessed was a knife, and both his captors had guns.

They had ridden another hour before they came to a pair of tree-studded hills where a ribbon-like trail ran up the side of a slope heading south. Their winded horses could only navigate it at a walk, and even then they encountered difficult places where one horse or the other had to scramble to keep its footing. Slocum followed the trail with his eyes, seeing where it appeared to pass over the top of the ridge in front of them. Surrounded by trees, the pathway was barely visible in some spots where it wound around slabs of bald rock or turned to avoid a climb too steep for any animal other than a mountain goat. By the looks of things, not many people ventured to Guerrero by this route. Idly, he wondered what they would find when they got there. Pedro had told him Zambrano had only four *pistoleros* with him now.

One thing became abundantly clear riding up the side of this steep hill—there would be no possibility of a fast escape from Guerrero if Slocum found a way to free the girl while he was here. No horse on earth could manage terrain like this in a hard gallop.

"We are close to Guerrero now," Chico said over his shoulder. "You would be wise to make your offer in a polite way, or Luis will become angry."

"I'll try to remember that," Slocum replied, hoping the sarcasm in his voice wasn't too evident.

Chico gave him a mirthless grin. "If you do not remember, Luis will have you shot, Señor. Perhaps knowing this will help you remember."

Nothing more was said as they rode off the ridge down a very steep drop into a canyon. Slocum never doubted Chico's promise that Zambrano would order him executed should he neglect protocol. Again, he felt naked without his guns heading into a place where he must deal with five heavily armed bandits. A moment of carelessness when he entered his hotel room had cost him dearly, putting him at such a disadvantage that the only bargaining tool he had was an offer of ransom money. Dumb mistakes like his cost men their lives every day. He hoped this wasn't his day to learn life's most important and final lesson in survival.

At a fork in the valley floor, they came in sight of a town with a low adobe wall around it, typical of Mexican villages in the days when defense from Indians meant life or death.

Guerrero appeared to have only a few hundred citizens, perhaps less since many of its buildings looked vacant . . . crumbling stone and adobe walls and holes in some of the roofs.

They rode through an opening in Guerrero's walls, a gate guarded by a lone Mexican with a rifle. Forced to take a guess, Slocum would have figured fewer than a hundred people lived here, after a closer inspection. No more than fifteen small buildings occupied what limited space there was inside the walls, mostly dwellings, a few shops, and a market near the center of town.

Chico led them to the market building in Guerrero, the only one in the village having two floors. Windows across the front of upstairs rooms had small balconies overlooking the street. Chico rode to a hitch rail and swung down, motioning for Slocum to do likewise. To Slocum's left, Juanito got down off his chestnut without once taking his dark eyes off Slocum, as if he expected trouble from him at any moment.

"Inside," Chico said gruffly, aiming a thumb at a door into the front of the building, resting his other hand on the butt of his pistol. "Someone will inform Luis that we are here."

"Where's the boy Pedro?" Slocum asked, tying off his horse at the rail. "I'd like to see him before we meet with Zambrano."

Juanito spoke in a hoarse voice. "Go inside or I put a gun to your head and kill you now, gringo. The boy is no concern of yours."

Slocum gave Juanito an angry stare, then shook his head and started for the door. Without a gun he would be forced to take whatever cards were dealt him, including their threats and insults.

A bearded *pistolero* watched the entrance into the building as Slocum walked inside. He gave Slocum a disinterested look and then ignored him. Slocum entered a room full of small tables and chairs. Oil lamps hung from rafters above a dirt floor. No one was seated at any of the tables.

"Sit here," Chico ordered, indicating a table near a front window looking out on the street.

The place was quiet, making the sound of Slocum's boots the only noise when he walked over to the table and took a chair with his back to the wall. The room smelled faintly of stale beer and corn tortillas and other scents he couldn't readily identify. His chair was fashioned from tree limbs, covered with goatskin. The table was hand-hewn from rough planks, stained, initials carved in spots. Juanito came over to the wall and leaned against it so that he was close to Slocum's right shoulder. Chico said a few words in Spanish, then crossed the room and walked up a set of wood steps leading to the top floor.

Slocum folded his arms across his chest, leaning his chair back against the wall. He was about to meet Mexico's famous bandit Luis Zambrano, while being surrounded by *pistoleros,* all heavily armed. And he had no gun.

All of this, he thought, because of a beautiful woman named Amanda Drake up in Abilene. He hoped fate had not dealt him a losing hand over a woman this time.

16

A shadow fell across the floor just beyond a door frame into the next room. Slocum recalled what Tom Spence had said about Zambrano, that he was considered one of the worst border cutthroats in the north of Mexico, almost legendary for his ability to elude capture by the Mexico army. Tom wouldn't have handed out that kind of warning without plenty of justification, being marshal of a town like Laredo, one of the toughest places anywhere. Slocum leaned back in his chair waiting for Zambrano to appear, certain the bandit leader would try to test him, to get at the truth. Zambrano would expect a trick, a deception of some kind, as any careful man should. There would be hard questions, and maybe some bluffing, until the Mexican was sure Slocum's ransom offer was genuine.

A man filled the doorway, heavy shoulders almost too broad to allow him to enter the room. A coarse black beard covered half of a round face and fleshy jowls. Powerful hands dangled at his sides near a brace of pistols. His hair fell to his shoulders in neglected curls, making him appear even more menacing, a wild look that would be unsettling to men who lacked experience dealing with tough types. He wore leather leggings, a sleeveless cotton shirt badly soiled by food stains and sweat, and stovepipe boots almost touching his knees.

"*Quien es?*" the Mexican asked, wanting to know who Slocum was, directing his question to Juanito. By his demeanor, he was accustomed to having his way.

Juanito answered in Spanish. Although Slocum understood only a few of the words, it was clear Juanito was explaining why Slocum was in Guerrero.

Zambrano grunted, scowling, bushy eyebrows knitted together. A lengthy silence followed while he sized up Slocum without walking across the room. As Slocum was making his own appraisal of Zambrano, he heard a gun being cocked close by. He knew the sound was made by Juanito. To show he had no fear of the gun, Slocum did not turn his head to look at Juanito's pistol.

"Stand up, Luis is here," Juanito demanded, as he aimed his revolver at Slocum's skull.

Gambling that Juanito would not shoot him without orders to do so from Zambrano, Slocum sat still, meeting Zambrano's cold stare. "I'd be glad to stand up and shake hands with him when he comes over to talk to me," Slocum replied evenly.

Hearing this, Zambrano smiled crookedly, revealing a single gold tooth in the front of his mouth, yet there was no mistaking the smile for a sign of friendliness. "Are you brave, hombre? Or maybeso only loco. Have you no fear of a gun?"

Slocum merely shrugged, showing courage he didn't actually feel right then. "I don't figure he'll shoot me without orders from you, Luis. And I don't figure you'll have me shot until you hear what I have to say about giving you money for the girl you took prisoner in Abilene. The girl's sister wants her back and she's willing to pay."

Zambrano's expression did not visibly change. "How much money do you bring to pay for her?"

"I didn't bring any. I'm here to negotiate for her release, and if we can agree on terms, I'll bring the money across the Rio Grande and deliver it to you personally."

The bandit seemed to be thinking. "How much money will you give for this dark-hair American woman?"

"I've got a letter in my pocket from a bank in Laredo which authorizes me to offer five thousand dollars in gold for the safe return of Alice Drake to Texas. As soon as you bring her to a place we both agree on, I'll hand you the money and I'll take her back to Laredo."

"This place," Zambrano said, "where is this place you want me to take her?"

"Someplace close enough to the border so I can make sure you won't change your mind. Once I've paid for her, I intend to keep her."

Hearing this, Zambrano left the doorway and sauntered over to Slocum's table, glaring down at him, hooking his thick thumbs in his gunbelt. "Show me this letter," he said, making it sound as though he doubted its existence.

Slocum took the letter from his pocket, handing it to Luis in an envelope. "I can verify everything it says in that letter by sending a wire from the telegraph office in Sabinas. The offer is genuine. Amanda Drake wants her sister back and she'll pay five thousand dollars in American gold to get it done. The only conditions are that she is unharmed and that you bring her someplace close to the border. It's a straight-forward proposition."

Zambrano opened the letter, looked at it, and handed it to Chico. "Tell me what it say. Read it carefully," he warned.

Chico squinted at the paper in poor light, eyes following each line written in careful longhand. "It say this man is John Slocum and he have authority to offer five thousand dollars in American gold for the return of Miss Alice Drake to Laredo, in Texas, to be paid when she cross the Rio

Grande. It say telegraph sent to Laredo State Bank in Laredo will be answered by a Mr. Thomas Spence that this money will be paid to Luis Zambrano in gold coins.''

Zambrano cast a suspicious look at Chico, then at Slocum as he listened to the letter. "Letter say money paid when she cross Rio Grande. You say we meet close to border. Letter no say you give me gold before she cross river. Is no good, this letter.''

"It's the wording. All it means is that the money will be given to you when you bring her to a place we agree upon—''

"No bueno!'' Valdez shouted. "Letter must say we get money before woman cross river!''

"I can arrange to have that put in the message we get back from Laredo. If you'll send someone with me to the telegraph at Sabinas, I'll get you an answer stating the money will be paid as soon as we make the exchange, the girl for the gold.''

It was quickly evident there was something about the proposed arrangement Zambrano didn't like. "Words on piece of paper mean nothing, gringo. I must have proof there is gold. You bring this gold to me and I give you the woman. You come here. I count money. Then woman is yours.''

"I can't do that and you know why,'' Slocum protested. "It would be too dangerous for me to bring that kind of money down here, and then I'd have to ride more than a hundred miles to get back to the border. I don't know any of the back roads, and if the *federales* found me with the money or the girl, there'd be too many questions. And I'd be taking a risk that you might change your mind and take the girl back once I gave you the money. I want some assurances that I can get the girl safely across the river. It's just good business.''

Zambrano seemed to take offense over Slocum's remark,

with a narrowing of his eyelids. "You insult me, gringo, saying you think I cheat you, I take this money and keep woman."

Slocum felt trapped, yet he knew he had to insist upon a meeting place near the border or there was a real chance the bandit would double-cross him. Doing some fast thinking, he said, "It wasn't my idea. Amanda Drake said she'd only pay the money if she had assurances that her sister would be released close to the Rio Grande. Otherwise, she won't allow the bank to give me the gold. It probably has as much to do with the fact that she does not trust *me*. She may be worried that I'll ride off with her money and she'll never see her sister again. I'm only acting as an agent, so to speak. Amanda Drake doesn't know me. We only met a few days ago up in Abilene. I was hired to negotiate the girl's release. I came down from Abilene to see if I could contact you and make the arrangements."

His answer seemed to satisfy Zambrano for the moment; however, some doubts lingered. "Maybeso you take the gold and keep it for yourself, gringo. How much this woman pay you to come here?"

It was time to tell part of the truth. "I get half of what you're being paid, more or less. About two thousand dollars."

"I think you lie to me," Zambrano said, scowling.

A silence followed. Slocum said, "I have no stake in this. I came here for the money, to make a payday. If you're interested in the proposition, I'll telegraph the bank in Laredo from Sabinas and have the gold ready for an exchange. If you're not, I'll ride back to Laredo and wire Amanda Drake that the deal wasn't satisfactory, that you've decided to keep the girl. It don't make any difference to me. I can't get paid unless I get the girl back to Texas alive. And there's one more thing. I need to talk to the girl, so I can wire Amanda that she's alive and okay."

Zambrano had been listening closely to everything Slocum said, and when he finished describing what the conditions for an exchange would be, Zambrano put the palm of his right hand on the butt of one pistol.

"Two thousand for you. Five thousand dollars for me. I have the woman. You have nothing, Señor Slocum. The woman in Abilene pays you too much for coming here."

Not sure what to say, Slocum replied, "It's the deal I was offered. I didn't set the price."

"Is not enough," Zambrano snarled.

Chico chuckled, looking at Zambrano. "This gringo make too much money. If you say the word, Juanito will shoot him. He is one dead gringo, *verdad*?"

"*Es verdad,*" Zambrano agreed, nodding once.

"I didn't set the price," Slocum told them again.

Zambrano cast a wary look out the window to the street. "I am an honorable man. You tell the sister of this girl that I sell her for ten thousand dollars in gold."

"That's too high," Slocum said, wagging his head. "Amanda will pay five thousand. Not a dime more . . ."

"She pay ten thousand," Zambrano said.

"She won't do it," Slocum argued.

"Then her sister will die," Zambrano promised. "You send a telegraph message to her. Tell her pay me ten thousand in gold or I cut the woman's throat."

"That doesn't leave anything for me," Slocum said, his mind racing. Would Zambrano kill the girl?

"Is your problem," the bandit said. He gave Chico a look. "Take Señor Slocum to *la oficina telegrafica.* Let him send this message to Laredo, or to Abilene. Pay ten thousand dollars in gold for the girl or I will kill her, *prontito*!"

Chico shook his head. "*Sí, Jefe.* I will see that this is the message Señor Slocum sends from Sabinas."

"*Bueno,*" Zambrano said, stepping back, telling Slocum their conversation was ended.

Juanito nudged the base of Slocum's skull with the barrel of his pistol. "Get up, gringo. We ride back to Sabinas. You say words Luis tell you to say, or I kill you. *Comprende?*"

"I understand," Slocum muttered, pushing back his chair. "I don't think Amanda Drake will agree to it, but I'll send the message anyway."

Zambrano wore a satisfied look. "The sister of this girl will agree to pay ten thousand dollars," he said, sounding very sure of it. "Tell her I will kill her if she say no."

Slocum stood up, remembering Pedro. "I'd like to see the boy who brought you my message. Just to make sure he's okay. I didn't give him anything for coming here. He didn't do anything wrong."

"The boy is dead," Zambrano said. "I ordered one of my men to shoot him. He was a traitor. He tell his cousin, Raul, that he help a gringo come to Sabinas to kill me for the rewards. I had no choice, Señor Slocum. I must have men killed who tell others where we are."

Slocum stiffened. "The kid didn't mean any harm. No reason to shoot him like that."

Zambrano grinned, showing off his gold tooth. "You no understand, gringo. Many people in Mexico try to find me. If anyone tells where to look for me, *los federales* or the bounty hunters from across the river will come. I gave the order to have this boy shot. His own cousin, Raul, was ordered to kill him. All the people of Guerrero saw his execution. They will tell others what will happen to anyone who comes to Mexico telling where we hide from *los federales* or bounty hunters from the north."

Hearing that Pedro had been executed by his own cousin, Slocum made angry balls of his fists. "The kid knew nothing," he said. "You shot an innocent kid who only came here bearing my message."

Zambrano had a gleam in his dark eyes when he replied,

"I do not shoot innocent people, Señor Slocum. The boy came here. He could have led *los federales* or hired killers to me. No one is to come to Guerrero, or to any other place where we hide from our enemies. This boy you call Pedro knew this. He came knowing he risked his own life."

Slocum lowered his head. Pedro had been killed delivering a message at Slocum's request. It was mindless, to shoot the boy for bringing an offer of ransom. Now Pedro's death hung heavy on Slocum's conscience.

"We go now," Chico said, motioning Slocum to the front door by inclining his head.

"I'll send that wire," Slocum said quietly, giving Zambrano a look. "Ten thousand is too much to ask for the girl, but I'll tell Miss Drake it's your price. Now let me get a look at her sister."

Zambrano aimed a thumb toward an adjoining room. Slocum went to the doorway with Juanito close at his heels, his gun in Slocum's back.

There, on a lumpy mattress, lay a brunette girl with her wrists tied to bedposts. A deep purple bruise colored one of her cheeks. She appeared to be asleep. But she was breathing.

"Now go," Zambrano said. "And tell her sister the price is ten thousand, or I will slit her throat when I'm done with her."

Slocum turned away, trudged past Chico to the door, and walked out as a late afternoon sun slanted into the village. Mounting his horse, he made himself a promise. If he could, he would make Luis Zambrano pay dearly for having the boy put to death.

17

Justin Davis spoke to Buck Jones as he, Joe Sikes, and Lucky Starnes headed east out of Sabinas with a young Mexican *vaquero* covered by Joe's pistol, one of Pedro's companions who'd tried to jump Slocum in the dark south of the little cantina on the road to Aguas Calientes.

"A fine piece of luck," Davis said, "findin' this Meskin boy who saw John Slocum pass by on his way to Sabinas. Slocum has it figured he'll earn that reward from Miss Amanda for gettin' her sister back. Well, boys, we're just about to put an end to Slocum's plans."

"But what about that bunch of *bandidos*?" Buck asked as they rode into a ravine following the road to Guerrero. "We done been told this Luis Zambrano is one mean son of a bitch, an' he's got a bunch with him nearly as bad."

"We ain't exactly tinhorns when it comes to shootin'," was Davis's reply. "Most Meskins ain't got much nerve when lead starts flyin' towards 'em. We'll shoot hell out of 'em an' grab that girl, makin' us a five-thousand-dollar payday."

Joe Sikes spoke up. "It was *real* lucky we run across this boy Arturo. He's the one who's been findin' out which way they went ever since we found him. We woulda never

126

knowed where to look in this hellhole if it wasn't for him.''

Davis chuckled. ''He ain't doin' it 'cause he wants to, Joe. Havin' this gun aimed at him is keepin' him honest.''

Buck gave the sky a thoughtful look. ''We can ride around this town Guerrero an' get the lay of things first. Then we sneak in at night an' find out where they've got Miss Amanda's sister hid.''

''I 'spect there'll be plenty of shootin','' Lucky offered quietly. ''Let's hope we all get out of this alive to spend our shares of that money.''

''You worry too damn much, Lucky,'' Davis said. ''We've been in tough scrapes with plenty of experienced gunhands. Just kill every Meskin you see an' you can't go wrong.''

''It's that Slocum feller I'm worried about,'' Lucky added, looking over at Davis. ''He damn sure got the drop on you quick as a wink.''

Davis scowled. ''I wasn't ready for him. Hell, I'd already shot down that loudmouth kid. Didn't expect that bastard Slocum to grab my gun hand like he done. I was waitin' for him to make his draw.''

''We'll kill him too if he gets in the way,'' Buck said. ''He may be dead already, one man goin' up against a gang of Meskin *pistoleros*. He's gotta be a damn fool.''

Davis ground his teeth together, recalling the incident in Abilene. ''He's gonna be a dead damn fool if I find him. You can bet your bankroll on that.''

''I'll kill him if I get him in my rifle sights,'' Lucky said with assurance. ''I hardly ever miss with a Winchester an' you boys know it's the truth.''

Davis checked their backtrail. ''Main thing we gotta do right now is watch out for Meskin soldiers. They'll be wantin' to know what we're doin' down here, carryin' all these pistols an' rifles an' shotguns.''

Joe said, "I hear tell if they put you in jail down here, it's damn near impossible to get out."

"We ain't broke no laws yet," Buck observed.

"Not till we find that Drake girl," Davis said. "Besides, we done been told this Luis Zambrano is wanted by the *federales* as well as the law in Texas. Hell, we'll be doin' everybody a favor if we find him an' kill him."

The boy, Arturo, understood most of what was being said in English. "Zambrano be very hard to kill, Señores. He is very fast with his *pistolas*."

"We'll test him," Davis promised.

Lucky added, "He may not get the chance to use his pistols if I draw a bead on him first with this Winchester. I'll blow his head clean off his neck."

Davis turned to Arturo. "What about the others with this Zambrano?"

"Two are very fast also. Juanito Alvarez is quick and he never sleeps."

"Who's the other one?"

"Raul Morales is very fast. Chico Obregon is big and he may be slow, but he is always careful. He will also be hard to kill."

They crossed a dry arroyo where the ruts in the road were deeper. Joe's horse began to cough in the caliche dust kicked up by the other horses' heels.

"It don't matter about any of 'em," Davis said after a bit of thought. "When a bullet hits the right spot, there ain't a man on earth who don't bleed an' die. And that damn sure includes Slocum."

A blazing afternoon sun soon had their horses lathered as they rode closer to Guerrero, but Justin Davis paid no attention to the heat. His mind was set on revenge for the humiliation he had suffered at the hands of John Slocum, the fancy-dressed dude from Denver with the cross-pull holster. Davis promised himself he wouldn't be so careless the next time he faced Slocum. His plan was simply to gun him down at the first opportunity.

"Miss Amanda's liable to be more than a little grateful if we bring her sister back," Joe said. "What I mean by that is, she might do more'n pay us the reward money."

"She don't buck-jump no ordinary cowboys," Lucky said. "In case you forgot, she owns the Silver Spur an' that ain't no cheap joint."

Davis considered it. "She might at that, boys, if a man put it to her just right."

"An' there's another thing," Buck told them. "Little Miss Alice ain't hard to look at. The way the story goes, that slick gambler Carl Smith taught her how to use laudanum an' she got to likin' it real good. After we get her back from this Zambrano feller, an' take care of Mr. Fancy John Slocum, we all might take us a little ride on Miss Alice. If she's drugged all to hell on that laudanum, she'd never know we had our way with her, most likely."

"It's somethin' else to think about," Davis agreed. "But first, we gotta find Zambrano an' kill him an' his gunmen, an' do the same to Slocum. We're a long way from bein' ready to take on a woman just now."

"Look yonder," Joe said, pointing to a distant ridge lined with mesquites.

"What is it, Joe?" Davis asked, squinting in the sun's harsh glare.

"A couple of riders. One wearin' a big sombrero. Looked for a minute like they was headed straight for us, till they rode out of sight in them trees."

"Prob'ly only a couple of Meskins cowhands," Buck said as he too watched the empty ridge.

"Maybe we oughta play it safe anyhow," Lucky said, drawing his Winchester from its saddle boot, jacking a shell into the firing chamber.

"Just so it ain't none of them damn *federales*," Joe said

in a quiet voice. "I sure as hell don't aim to spend no time in a Meskin jail."

"Let's pull off this road an' wait for 'em," Davis suggested.

"That'd be real smart," Buck agreed, reining his horse off the wagon ruts.

Davis, and Lucky followed Buck into a thicket of scrub mesquite bushes. Joe ushered Arturo off the road ahead of him with a cocked pistol.

"We'll wait for 'em here," Davis said, drawing his own rifle out.

"Could be we're all gettin' too damn jumpy," Lucky said as he readied his rifle near his shoulder.

Davis turned to the Mexican boy. "Keep your eyes on the top of them hills, kid. Tell me if you recognize either one of them riders when we see 'em again."

"*Sí, Señor,*" Arturo stammered.

"And if you make a mistake," Davis continued, "I'm gonna blow a hole plumb through you."

"I will look very closely, Señor."

Arturo turned in the saddle quickly a quarter of an hour later. "The big one is Chico Obregon, the *pistolero* who rides with Zambrano. I do not recognize the other one, but he is gringo, *norteamericano.*"

"It could be Slocum," Davis said, trying to see the two riders more clearly.

"Why the hell would he be ridin' with one of Zambrano's gunmen when he's after the girl, same as us?"

"Hard to say," Davis replied.

"Wait'll they get a little closer an' I'll kill 'em both," Lucky said, sighting along the barrel of his Winchester. "Give me another two hundred yards an' it'll be an easy shot, like shootin' ducks in a barrel."

"Sure hope there ain't no *federales* close enough to hear any shootin'," Joe remarked.

Davis's jaw went hard. "If it's John Slocum we're gonna kill him, an' I don't give a damn if the whole Mexican army hears us do it."

"Just be quiet, boys," Lucky said, standing in his stirrups for the best view of the roadway. "I'll drop 'em both so quick they won't know what hit 'em, only you gotta be quiet so they don't know we're here waitin' for 'em."

The men sat in silence. Two riders came around a far bend in the trail, and now Davis could see them well.

"It *is* Slocum," he whispered.

"*Sí, Señor,*" Arturo said softly, "and the big one is Chico Obregon."

"Today's our lucky day," Davis said under his breath as he brought his rifle to bear on one target, the man in the Stetson hat, John Slocum.

"We ain't killed 'em yet," Buck reminded.

"Shut up!" Lucky hissed, steadying his rifle. "Don't say another word till I kill 'em."

"They're as good as dead now," Davis whispered. "I'm gonna blow John Slocum straight to Hell for what he done to me."

18

Slocum heard the rifle crack. The big Mexican riding next to him flinched as both horses spooked when they heard the loud explosion.

A spurt of blood flew from Chico's back. His pinto lunged just as Slocum dove off one side of the grulla to the ground, landing on his chest.

"Ayiii!" Chico cried as he toppled backward, rolling off the cantle of his saddle amid a spray of crimson coming from a spot between his shoulders.

Another rifle blasted before Chico thudded heavily on the caliche, his arms and legs landing limply, yet he continued to scream in pain.

Slocum belly-crawled over to the Mexican, figuring they'd run headlong into a *federale* ambush designed to end Zambrano's bandit career. Slocum jerked his Colt Peacemaker from Chico's belt as both horses galloped away from the noises into thick mesquite brush lining both sides of the rutted road between Guerrero and Sabinas.

I'm out in the open, Slocum thought, slithering as fast as he could toward a clump of yucca fans that would offer nothing more than a momentary hiding place and no protection at all from flying bullets.

He made it to the yuccas out of breath, peering between the blades to see how many men were shooting at them. The shots had taken him completely by surprise while he was figuring a way to make a move on Chico with his bowie knife.

The crackle of more gunfire gave him a rough count of the men ambushing them, four or five guns, no more, unless only a few were doing the shooting.

I've got to get my hands on a rifle, he told himself, coming to his hands and knees to make a dash into the brush to reach the horses.

A gun thundered as he ran in a low crouch to the closest thicket of mesquites. A bullet whined over his head, snapping off a mesquite limb.

He caught a glimpse of the pinto and the grulla a few dozen yards deeper into the thicket.

Keeping low, he hurried toward the animals without firing an answering shot at the men he judged were part of a *federale* patrol who kept blasting away from a mesquite grove almost three hundred yards to the northwest.

"Easy, boy," he said to the pinto gelding as he crept up on the horse. Chico's rifle was booted to his empty, blood-stained saddle.

Slocum pulled the Winchester, levered a shell into the firing chamber, and quickly opened one saddlebag to look for more cartridges.

He found a half-empty box of .44 rifle shells and gave a sigh of relief. Then he moved over to the grulla and tied its reins to a low limb. Slocum didn't plan to remain afoot for long, just long enough to find out how many *federales* he faced when he made his escape on Tom Spence's grulla.

The gunfire died down, and then stopped altogether.

Slocum filled his pockets with rifle cartridges and then crept among the trees, moving toward the *federales* to see if they were attempting to encircle him, or merely waiting in ambush for him to show himself.

I won't go far from my horse, he thought, dodging back and forth among the mesquites. It may come down to a horse race if there are too many of them for me to handle.

Chico's cries softened to groans, and Slocum knew the *pistolero* was dying slowly, painfully. One of the rifle shots had been meant for Slocum, a little high and wide of its mark, and he was now thankful for the *federales'* bad aim, even though one had been good enough to drop Chico with his first shot.

At the edge of a small clearing he caught sight of a horse and rider, and to his surprise the man was not a Mexican soldier. A cowboy in a dusty gray Stetson rode cautiously along the edge of the roadway toward Chico, a rifle cocked and held up to his shoulder.

Then Slocum saw another horseman, and he recognized him at once.

"Justin Davis," he whispered. "The son of a bitch came after me, or the reward. Or both."

He lifted the Winchester and steadied his aim on Justin Davis, remaining hidden behind the trunk of a mesquite until he was certain of his shot.

Slocum nudged the trigger. The roar of Chico's rifle made Davis's horse lunge, but not before the bullet Slocum fired at Davis tore through his belly.

"Yaaaa!" Davis bellowed as the force of impact ripped him from the saddle. He went spinning toward the ground, tossing his rifle in the air.

Slocum fired at the other rider before Davis struck the caliche. His slug caught the gunman wearing the gray cowboy hat in the throat, snapping his head back at almost the same moment his horse reared, dumping him out of the saddle before the roan gelding galloped away.

Both Davis and his companion were dead or mortally

wounded, Slocum knew, but by the number of shots he'd heard when the ambush had started, there were others.

Then he heard the sounds of horses farther to the north, and saw three men, two cowboys and a young Mexican boy, ride their horses out of a dense mesquite forest.

The men spurred their horses away from the fight instead of riding toward Slocum.

"Not much nerve, with Davis down," Slocum muttered as he straightened up behind the tree.

Walking cautiously, he made his approach toward Davis and his partner, to make sure both men were permanently out of the battle. He kept an eye on the departing riders until they rode over the top of a hill.

He came up to Justin Davis first, staring down into the man's pain-filled eyes.

Davis saw him, blinking furiously while blood leaked out of his wound onto the ground.

"Not very smart, Davis," Slocum said.

"You bastard," Davis choked, swallowing blood, a sure indication that Slocum's slug had pierced a lung. "We had you cold."

"Not cold enough," Slocum replied. "Besides, this is real hot country we're in."

"You've got luck," Davis said, groaning.

"It's more than luck, asshole."

"You can't be that good, or that lucky. I should have killed you up in Abilene."

"You never had a chance and you knew it."

"Like hell. I was watchin' your gun hand."

"That was your first mistake, Davis."

"I coulda killed you. I'm faster."

"It's an easy claim to make," Slocum told him. "But it's harder to prove. Talking is one thing. Getting something done the way you want it is another."

Davis closed his eyes a moment. "I hope this Luis Zambrano finds you an' blows your fuckin' head off.''

"He'll have a chance to find me," Slocum said softly, after a glance up and down the roadway. "In fact, I'm gonna go lookin' for him."

"You went an' killed Lucky to boot," Davis said, his voice dropping to a whisper as blood loss weakened him. "He should have aimed for you first, 'stead of that big Meskin."

"Lucky don't sound like a very good name for him," Slocum remarked, looking over at the other wounded gunman. "I'd say his nickname oughta been Unlucky. He's dying. I put a bullet through his neck. Don't figure he can breathe all that well."

Davis opened his eyes and stared up at Slocum again, only now his eyeballs had a dull glaze over them. "Tell me one thing, Slocum." He coughed before he could continue, spitting up pink foam. "How come you didn't shoot me up in Abilene when you had the chance?"

"Too easy."

"Too easy?" Davis didn't understand.

"All I had to do was pull and put a hole in the same place where you've got one now."

"Nobody's that fast."

Slocum was growing tired of the banter. "I'd stay a while longer and debate the point with you, only I've got business in Guerrero."

"I hope they kill you, you rotten bastard."

"I'm sure they're gonna try. Over the years, even back in the war, plenty of men have tried. I've got a few holes in my skin for their efforts, but nobody's been able to get it done so far."

"I'll see you in Hell, Slocum."

"Maybe," he replied, turning away to inspect the condition of the man Davis called Lucky. "But your place has already been reserved in the Devil's kitchen. Adios, Mr. Davis. Have a nice long sleep.''

He ambled over to Lucky and found the man unconscious, with so much loss of blood there was no way he could survive. The red ants had already come to feed on his blood, crawling over his skin, devouring his flesh.

Slocum picked up Lucky's rifle, for it was a model '73 Winchester like his own and he figured he could trust its sights more than the older model Chico carried.

He trotted off to find his grulla and head back for the village of Guerrero, where some unfinished business with Luis Zambrano was waiting for him.

It had been a close shave, this ambush by Davis and his men, and Slocum knew he'd been fortunate to survive it without so much as a scratch.

He paused when he came to Chico. The big Mexican was dead, his face and chest wound swarming with blowflies.

''You had it coming,'' Slocum told the corpse, as if the man could hear him.

He found the grulla, and took Chico's pinto as a spare mount for the girl, if he were able to arrange a deal with Zambrano to ransom her. He had to have a telegram from the Laredo bank with a statement to the effect that ten thousand dollars, not five thousand, would be delivered to Slocum to pay for Alice's release somewhere near the border.

He understood how it would have to be done. By wiring Tom Spence, telling him of Zambrano's demands, Slocum could ask Tom to send a phony wire back to Sabinas authorizing the payment of ten thousand, signed fictitiously by the Laredo State Bank. It was a ploy that stood some chance of working, but with several major difficulties. Slocum had to explain what happened to Chico when he returned to Guerrero with the false telegram, blaming it on bounty hunters. And then, if Zambrano agreed to accept the

ten thousand close enough to the border to turn it into a
horse race, Slocum had to find a way to fool the Mexican
bandit with half the amount of gold just long enough to
make a run for the border with Alice.

"None of this is gonna be easy," he said as he dragged
Chico's heavy body off the road into the brush.

It was unlikely the surviving bounty hunters who came
with Davis would go to the *federales* in Sabinas to report
what had happened, since American bounty hunters were
not welcome in most parts of Mexico. But there was a
chance he would have a run-in with a *federale* patrol somewhere along the way, either heading into Sabinas, or on the
way back with the telegram from Tom.

"It'll take some explaining," he muttered, leaving Justin
Davis and unlucky Lucky as buzzard bait right where they
fell.

He mounted the grulla and led Chico's pinto off toward
Sabinas, feeling somewhat better about things now. He was
armed again, and with enough firepower he could handle
most any event if something went wrong.

19

It was dark by the time he reached Sabinas. Crossing the hills had worn his horses down, and now the grulla traveled with its head lowered, gaunt-flanked, needing water and rest. All the way back, when Slocum allowed his mind to wander, he thought about Pedro being executed by his cousin for nothing more than bringing a message to Zambrano. Several times, remembering the boy, Slocum made a vow to make Zambrano and Raul pay for murdering an innocent kid whose only crime had been carrying an offer of ransom money in Slocum's behalf. He wondered how he would explain Pedro's fate to Señor Villareal at the ranch, and too, if the boy had any family to grieve for him. It hadn't seemed wrong then to offer Pedro a few silver dollars for riding to Zambrano's hideaway merely to inform him of the ransom money, but the job has cost Pedro his life and Slocum was to blame.

As before, Slocum rode into the city by back routes, avoiding main thoroughfares where he might be seen by *federale* patrols. A few dogs barked when the horses trotted down dark streets in quiet neighborhoods, but otherwise his arrival in Sabinas went unnoticed.

By circling the heart of town, he approached the telegraph office from the north. The little building was dark, appearing to be closed for the night. Slocum rode to the rear by way of an alley, then he climbed down from his saddle at a door leading into the back of the office.

Slocum's muscles were stiff after so many hours aboard his horse. He knocked on the door softly, after making sure no one had seen him in the dark alley.

"*Quien es?*" a small voice asked from inside.

"I need to send a very important telegram, for which I will pay extra money in silver," Slocum replied.

The door opened. The old man Slocum had seen in the telegraph office the day before peered out into the darkness.

The old man stepped aside to allow him to enter, after Slocum showed him a handful of silver dollars. A lantern was lit, revealing they were in a tiny bedroom. The telegraph operator carried his lantern into a front room where his telegraph key and generator sat on a desk.

"What do you wish to say, and where do you want the message sent?" the old man asked in near-perfect English, picking up a stub of a pencil, holding it above a piece of foolscap near the spot where he put his lamp.

"I want it sent to Laredo, Texas, in care of Tom Spence. I want you to say this, that the Laredo State Bank must send a return wire agreeing to pay ten thousand dollars in gold for the . . . merchandise I was sent down here to buy for Miss Drake. Ten thousand in gold is the price, and Tom must send the wire himself, signing the bank's name to it. Ask to have an answer wired back here as soon as possible. Sign my name to it, John Slocum."

The old man wrote slowly, and it required several minutes for Slocum's message to be transcribed properly. Then the old man turned a hand crank on his generator a number of times, sat down, and tapped his telegraph key, only a few strokes before he paused.

"They will answer in Monterrey if the line is working.

This message must be sent to Monterrey first, then to Laredo. It will take time, a few hours.''

"Tell me when the message has been sent. I'll wait at that little cantina across from the plaza for the answer to come. You bring it to me there. Tell no one about this . . . no one!'' Slowly, Slocum counted out ten silver dollars and placed them in front of the old man.

The old man agreed silently, watching his telegraph key. A short time later the key started to click, then stopped. "The line is open to Monterrey. I will send this message right away. When the answer comes I bring it to Cantina El Matador.''

Slocum left by the rear door. He walked out quietly, after carefully surveying the alleyway for any sign of activity. Once aboard his horse, he reined to the northeast, making another circle around the business district of Sabinas, keeping to deeper shadows wherever he could.

Near the eastern edge of Sabinas he came to a squat adobe shed sitting off by itself in a mesquite grove with an empty pole corral behind it. Slocum swung down and led the horses inside the corral to keep them from being seen by passersby in the moonlight.

Tugging his hat low to cover his face, Slocum headed for the plaza and the Cantina El Matador, where he'd spent one afternoon waiting for Pedro's return. Just thinking about Pedro again made him angry.

Slocum had been worrying about what the return wire would say, and he hoped Tom would send a reply agreeing to Zambrano's price, with a forged signature from the bank. Tom should understand that what mattered most was getting Alice Drake close to the border by any ruse. Slocum had told the telegraph operator all he dared say about what he intended to do, hoping that the silver would still his tongue about the message.

He strolled into the quiet cantina, where a few drinkers

sat at small tables or stood at the bar. When he walked in, some patrons exchanged polite nods with him as if to say his presence did not disturb them.

"Tequila," Slocum told a plump young waitress. She hurried off to bring back a bottle of tequila and a dish of cut limes.

He poured a drink, taking a slice of lime, wishing with all his heart that young Pedro Gonzalez hadn't lost his life. It saddened him greatly that the boy was killed. He'd kept his temper in check about as long as he could. Biting into a lime, he tasted its bitter juice and tried to keep from remembering Pedro. Slocum's father had had a favorite saying he often quoted to his sons when the family trait called Slocum temper got out of hand: "Don't get mad. Get even." And that was precisely what John Slocum intended to do at the first opportunity.

The old man did not come to the cantina until well after midnight. He spoke to no one, then motioned Slocum to come outside. He handed Slocum a folded piece of paper. Slocum read the telegraph message in light from a cantina window.

"John. Amount asked is agreed. You return at once. Pick up ten thousand in gold coin. Someone from the bank will ride with you to the place of exchange, to ensure the interests of Miss Amanda Drake. Signed, Spence Thomas, Laredo State Bank."

He hurried to the shed where the horses were tied. Slocum carried a fresh bottle of tequila. He was dreading another long ride back through rough country to reach Guerrero. He meant to show Zambrano the wire, explain what happened to Chico at the hands of bounty hunters, and then arrange a meeting place as close to the border as he could to make the exchange . . . the girl for the money.

Needing sleep, he mounted Chico's pinto to give the grulla a rest and reined out of the corral. A sky full of stars and a slice of new moon showed him the way out of Sabinas back to the old wagon road to Guerrero.

He allowed himself a small sigh of relief. At least Tom had known what to do and what to say in the return telegram. And one more thing seemed fairly clear in Tom's message . . . the part about a representative of the bank accompanying the money to the point of exchange. Slocum was sure he knew who that man would be.

"You'll make a lousy-lookin' banker, Tom," Slocum said as he heeled the pinto to a trot. "I hope like hell you can fool Luis Zambrano into thinking you're a man who handles money for a living."

The offer made Slocum realize what a friend Tom Spence truly was.

20

Slocum rode through the opening in the adobe wall at Guerrero just before dawn, after pushing the pinto gelding as
hard as he dared. The gate into the village was unguarded.
He rode to the front of the two-story building where the
girl was being kept and swung down to tie off both horses.
Leaving the rifle in its saddle boot so as not to appear
threatening, he walked into the darkened room without seeing anyone. It puzzled him why Zambrano had no one
guarding the place.

He heard a swishing noise behind him too late, then a
heavy object struck the back of his head. As he sank to the
floor he lost consciousness.

He awoke to find himself bound hand and foot, gagged,
unable to move. At first, still groggy, he fought his restraints until he realized the futility of it. Strips of rawhide
bound his legs and wrists. A foul-tasting rag had been
stuffed into his mouth, tied there by a faded red bandanna.
Slowly, his mind cleared and he remembered events before
he was knocked unconscious. He had walked into a black
room and then someone had hit him from behind.

He examined his surroundings. He was in a small room

made of cut stones and mortar, windowless, a sliver of sunlight at the bottom of a heavy wood door. A dirt floor. No furniture or other objects. Had Juanito been the one who struck him from behind and then tied him up here?

Struggling, his head pounding, Slocum managed to sit up with his knees bent. His wrists were tied in front of him rather than behind his back. Blood seeped from his skin where the bindings cut into his flesh.

He suddenly remembered the knife in his boot, but his hopes fell when he discovered it was gone. And slowly, the hopelessness of his situation began to sink in. He was a prisoner, bound hand and foot, probably awaiting an order for his execution by a member of the bandit gang. They would kill him the same way they'd killed Pedro. Unless he could talk his way out of this mess, he was most likely spending the last few hours of his lifetime now. He'd been in dozens of close scrapes in the last twenty-odd years, and he'd always found some way out just in the nick of time. But how could he get out of this?

Despair closed in on him. He had never been one to give up hope, yet this time, things looked their blackest. In all his memory he couldn't recall being in a situation like this where he had no options, no choices, no way out. He'd fought his way out of plenty of tight spots, but always there had been his weapons to rely on, his skill with firearms to equalize long odds when they stood against him. Even when he faced an enemy with nothing but his fists, he'd found a way to win the upper hand. But now, with his hands and feet tied together, he was utterly defenseless and at the mercy of Zambrano and his men.

I can't give up now, he thought. I'll find a way to get my hands free . . . somehow.

By inching backward a little at a time, he reached the back wall of his prison and rested against it. The greasy rag in his mouth was making him sick to his stomach, but the knot in the bandanna was too tight and he couldn't loosen it. The effort to move backward to the wall had made his head throb with pain. He found he was slightly dizzy. As he rested, his mind raced to find some way to convince the bandit leader that he was worth more alive than dead. Without him there would be no ransom money paid, but would Zambrano listen to logic? Or would he simply put him to death the way he had the boy. . . .

Closing his eyes, Slocum considered every possibility, what he might say to Zambrano to keep him from killing him. He had the telegram guaranteeing the ten thousand dollars. Surely the greedy bandit would make a try to collect so much money. Slocum hoped Zambrano had the telegram now, for it was missing from his shirt pocket.

Damn the luck, he thought when he couldn't come up with an answer to his dilemma that stood much chance of working. Then, in a moment of reflection, he knew it wasn't luck that had done him in—he'd been careless going into his hotel room that day and this was the price to be paid for it.

He'd been dozing when he heard someone unlocking the door, and suddenly, he came wide awake. Two Mexicans in broad sombreros entered his room. He recognized one immediately. Juanito looked down at him with pure hatred in his eyes. The other man was tall and muscular, young, hardly more than twenty, with a dark mustache and a clean-shaven chin.

Juanito walked over to Slocum, his boots making a grinding noise on the dirt floor. *"Idiota,"* he snarled. "You will die for what you did, gringo, for killing Chico."

Slocum mouthed a denial. The rag stuffed in his cheeks prevented his words from being heard by either man.

The younger Mexican walked slowly across the room. He stared at Slocum for a moment, then drew back a booted foot and swung a vicious kick at Slocum's legs. The blow landed, glancing off his thigh, the result of poor aim.

"*Bastardo!*" the younger man cried, grimacing.

Juanito laughed dryly. "When Luis comes from the room with the girl he will order your execution, gringo. *Mañana,* tomorrow, you will die before our guns! The only reason I did not kill you last night was the gold. Luis wants this gold you say you pay for the woman." He gave Slocum a haughty glare, turned, and started for the door. "*Vamos,* Raul. Let the gringo think about the bullets after we get his gold, if this is the wish of Luis."

The other man grinned. "*Sí,* Juanito. Soon he dies, when we get the gold. It will be good to see this gringo *bastardo* die for what he did to Chico." He turned on his heel and followed Juanito out the door.

The door was locked, then boots sounded moving away. When Slocum tried to swallow, he found he couldn't with the rag in his mouth. He remembered something Juanito had said, that Zambrano was with Alice now. Perhaps the pretty girl will buy me more time to figure a way out of here, he thought.

He rested his head on the wall, working his tongue so that most of the rag was balled on one side of his mouth and he could swallow. His wrists were hurting where the rawhide strips were cutting him. Taking a deep breath, he looked closely at the knots binding his hands. It would be impossible to untie those pieces of green cowhide, yet he might be able to untie the cord around his ankles and at least free his feet so he could stand.

One important bit of information had come from Juanito— that Zambrano wanted the gold. With the ransom as bait, it might still be possible to talk sense to Zambrano. Without Slocum to arrange the exchange, there would be no gold. Juanito seemed to understand this. Now all Slocum had to do was convince Zambrano that no ransom would be paid unless Slocum made the deal personally.

His fingers were numb as he went to work on the leather tied around his ankles. But the rawhide, still damp before curing, was impossible to budge. As wet cowhide dried it would contract, making his bindings even tighter. By morning his wrists would be bleeding profusely.

After a few more minutes of futile struggle with the rawhide he gave up, and rested his aching head against the stone wall. It was useless to try any longer.

Later, when he felt somewhat better, his stomach growled with hunger. He couldn't recall when he last ate a square meal. He was growing weaker, feeling sleepy, although the pain in his head had begun to subside.

A key entered the lock. Slocum opened his eyes. A man came into the room carrying a tin plate. He placed it on the floor in easy reach, then knelt down and spoke softly, barely above a whisper. "I am Raul." He untied the bandanna and took the rag from Slocum's mouth.

Slocum remembered him as the man who'd accompanied Juanito a few hours earlier, the one who'd kicked him. Somewhere in the back of his brain he knew he should recognize the name, yet his mind was still fuzzy from dozing.

He glanced down to the plate. A pile of beans in some sort of sauce filled a tortilla. He muttered, "Thanks," and reached for his food as Pedro spoke again.

"Pedro Gonzalez was my cousin."

Suddenly, Slocum was wide awake. "They told me you shot him yourself," he said quietly, searching Raul's face.

Raul nodded. "I was ordered to shoot Pedro for coming to Guerrero without sending a certain messenger from Sabinas. Pedro could not have known this and rode straight to the village, and that is forbidden by Luis. Someone must come from Sabinas to ask for permission to come. Pedro did not know and Luis ordered his death, as example to any others who dare to come here. He told me I must kill my own cousin or Luis said he would kill me. My heart has been breaking ever since.''

''I'm sorry about your cousin. I liked the boy. He died because of me, because of what I asked him to do. His death is on my conscience too.''

Now Raul glanced over his shoulder, making sure no one was listening outside. ''Tonight I will come for you. I will let you out of this room and give you the grulla horse and your guns. That is all I can do for you, Señor, but if you ride quickly to the Rio Grande, Luis will not send anyone across after you and you will be safe.''

Slocum felt immediate relief, although he wondered why Raul would take such a chance. ''I'll owe you my life, Raul.'' He thought about Alice. ''The girl . . . I need to find out if she's okay, and where she's being kept.''

''He keeps her upstairs at the cantina,'' Raul whispered. ''I know of no one who has seen her except Juanito. He guards her room at night, and when Luis is away.''

Slocum's mind raced. ''If you let me out tonight and give me a couple of guns, what are my chances of getting her out of that room and out of Guerrero?''

Raul frowned. ''It would be very dangerous, Señor. And you would have to kill Juanito, who is very fast with *una pistola,* and the noise from a gun would awaken Luis.''

Slocum felt his anger swell. He owed Juanito for a bump on his head. ''I'd almost enjoy killing that son of a bitch Juanito. If I had my knife, I might get it done quietly so there wouldn't be any gunshots. If you could find my Bowie knife, and my pistols, or any kind of gun, I might be able to get the girl out of that room and onto a horse before anybody is the wiser. We'd need two fast horses and some weapons, if we're to stand any chance of getting to the border ahead of Zambrano and the men he'll send after me.''

Raul was worried. "Juanito will be a very hard man to kill with a knife or a gun, Señor. He is *un hombre malo,* a bad one."

"You leave that up to me. If you can get me my knife and my guns, or any good pistol and a rifle, along with two fast horses, I'll handle the rest."

Raul said, "I will see what I can do. I will ask Jose to look for your knife and the *pistolas.* He is a guard at the gate into the city. Jose may be able to let you inside tonight, if no one else is watching. Many men have left Zambrano because of his empty promises, and there are only a few who are good with guns. Tonight will be your only chance to escape, Señor. Tomorrow more men are expected to join us from the south."

"I'm grateful for the offer of help. If you come to Laredo, I'll see to it that you and Jose are well paid. The girl has a sister who'll be very generous if you help me get her out of here."

Again, Raul looked to the open door. "We are growing tired of the broken promises," he said. "We do not get but very little of the money. All we do is rob *los ricos,* many rich people, so Zambrano can be rich. There are some who do not believe him any longer. We are not giving to the poor. We have become nothing more than *bandidos.*"

Slocum leaned forward. "For whatever reasons, I'm grateful that you're willing to help me escape."

Raul's face turned to stone. "I help you because of what Luis forced me to do to Pedro, Señor." He stood up and dusted off his knees. "We will come late tonight when everyone is asleep. I will ask Jose to find your guns and the knife, if he knows where Juanito keeps them. If he is unable to find your weapons, I will bring whatever I can. I will tell Jose that you need one more horse for the woman. One thing you can be sure of, Señor. Luis and Juanito will come after you. If they catch you, they will kill you."

"Ask Jose if there's a way I can get upstairs to the room where they keep the girl. If I can, I aim to take her with me and I'll take care of Juanito first."

"Do not worry, Señor. I will not shoot at you. While Luis is chasing you, I will make my own escape to the border."

Pedro left, closed the door, and locked it without saying more, leaving Slocum to his thoughts.

"I've got a fighting chance now," he told himself, reaching for the tortilla and beans, realizing that he was starving. With hope for an escape, his mind cleared.

He recalled that Chico had been carrying his Colt Peacemaker and his bellygun, and he'd been able to get his Colt back until Juanito knocked him unconscious. His rifle and shotgun had been in a sling on Juanito's saddle as they rode to Guerrero. Killing Juanito silently in order to get the girl downstairs might prove to be tricky, but it was possible if things went just right.

If he got the girl out of the village, there was still the difficult task of negotiating a dangerous trail across rugged hills in the dark. And finally, a horse race across the Mexican desert to the Rio Grande. On the surface it appeared to be an almost impossible escape to pull off. Everything, down to the very last detail, would have to work smoothly. And even then, he would be counting on a sizable amount of luck. The girl would probably be drugged on laudanum and he'd have trouble keeping her in a saddle at a hard gallop.

Eating the last of his tortilla and beans, he licked his fingers and thought about what he faced in the coming hours and days. He'd faced tough situations before. . . .

21

Judging by the lack of sunlight coming under the door, Slocum knew when night came to Guerrero. Now and then he heard noises: footsteps near the room where he was being kept, occasional sounds of horses off in the distance. Soon it grew quiet. There was nothing to do but wait for Raul and Jose while hoping nothing went wrong with their plans to set him free.

He felt somewhat better after his meager meal, and with the rag removed from his mouth he suffered less, although his wrists ached and bled as the rawhide dried, tightening. He wished he'd asked Raul to cut his bindings; however, it was the sort of thing that might give Raul's plan away should someone else come to check on their prisoner. Thus Slocum was forced to sit with his knees bent, resting against a stone wall, awaiting a slim chance to make his escape. Everything depended on Raul and his amigo, Jose.

Slocum remembered Raul's swift kick when he'd accompanied Juanito into the room, and now he understood why it had been a glancing blow, a deliberate effort on Raul's part to seem angry toward a gringo prisoner. It was good acting on Raul's part.

Slocum dozed again, allowing himself badly needed sleep. If he managed to get away from Guerrero, there would be no opportunity for sleep until he reached the Rio Grande. Zambrano's men would hound him all the way to the border.

He'd only been asleep a short time when he heard someone put a key into the lock. The door swung open. Light from a coal-oil lantern spilled into the room, briefly hurting Slocum's eyes. He blinked, and then he recognized the man holding the lantern. An inner voice told him something had gone wrong.

Juanito swaggered over near the wall and put his lamp on the floor a few feet from Slocum. He slowly drew a revolver from his gunbelt. A savage grin raised the corners of his mouth. "How does it feel, gringo, to know you will die very soon?"

"That ain't been decided yet," Slocum answered defiantly as his temper heated up. "Your leader wants that ten thousand in gold I can bring him. I don't figure he'll have me killed until he gets his hands on that money. He'll keep me alive because me and that girl are worth ten thousand dollars to him."

Juanito came a half step closer. "Someone else can trade the woman for the gold."

"Without me, there's no one who can tell the girl's sister she's still alive. She won't release any money without hearing from me that her sister is okay." Slocum watched Juanito's gun carefully to see if he meant to use it. "Zambrano will be mighty unhappy if something happens to me so he can't collect the gold. If I was you I'd be thinking about that. . . ."

Sudden anger wiped the grin off Juanito's face. He set his jaw, then swung the barrel of his pistol, striking a vicious blow across Slocum's left cheek.

Slocum tried to duck away from the gun much too

slowly, and when it struck him, his head was driven back against the wall. He tasted blood. His ears were ringing. Fearing another blow, he drew back as far as he could, hunkering down to make as small a target as possible.

"I should kill you now, saying to Luis that you tried to get away," Juanito spat, his feet spread apart as if he meant to come at Slocum again.

Slocum ran his tongue over his teeth slowly to see if any were broken. Blood filled his mouth from a cut inside his cheek. He said nothing else, watching Juanito.

Finally, Juanito straightened and holstered his gun. He took the lantern and moved to the door. "You will die, gringo," he promised. "Maybe soon or later, I will put a bullet through your heart." He closed the door and locked it.

Slocum listened to him walk away before he spat out a mouth full of blood. His eyelids narrowed. "Maybe you won't live long enough to get the chance, asshole," he whispered, clenching his teeth in quiet rage.

Nursing a sore cheek, he allowed his temper to cool. If he got the opportunity he didn't want anger to get in the way of his plan for revenge.

Slocum had all but given up hope that Raul and Jose were coming to let him out, figuring something had gone wrong. A noise alerted him that someone was close to the door. Then a key turned tumblers in the lock very softly, and light from the stars spilled through the doorway onto the floor.

A shadow crept toward him, and for a moment Slocum feared it was Juanito, coming back to kill him with a knife. But when he heard Raul's voice, he relaxed.

"Two horses are saddled." A knife blade went to work on his wrist bindings; then his ankles were freed. "Here is your knife. Your rifle and shotgun are with the horses. I give you my own pistol and bullets. Juanito has your guns hidden and Jose is not able to find them.''

Slocum was handed his Bowie knife and a gunbelt holding a Colt .44 and loops full of cartridges. He stood up and strapped on the gun before sheathing the knife in his boot. ''What about getting to the girl?'' he whispered. ''Will Jose let me go upstairs?''

Pedro hesitated. ''It will be very dangerous. Another guard is at the front, and Juanito is upstairs in front of the door to the room where she is kept.''

''I'll take the chance,'' he told Raul, eyeing the man's big sombrero. ''Let me have your sombrero. In the dark I'll look the same as everybody else. All you've got to do is show me where the horses are tied, and then take me to the back door of that cantina so Jose will let me in. I'll do the rest. If I can, I aim to silence Juanito with this knife so nobody will hear any ruckus. But if that don't work, I'll have to shoot my way out of the building and make a run for the horses.''

''*Buena suerte, Señor,*'' Raul said, wishing him good luck. ''Come. I will show you the horses, then we go to the door where Jose is guard.'' He took his sombrero off and handed it over to Slocum.

Slocum touched Raul's shoulder. ''Don't forget to come to Laredo as soon as you can. There's a sizable reward in this for you and Jose if me and the girl get back to Texas alive.''

''We will come, Señor. While the others are chasing you we will go northwest to Piedras Negras to cross the river. If all goes well we will see you in Laredo.''

''Come to the city marshal's office. Ask for Tom Spence. He will know if we made it okay. Now, show me those horses.'' With the sombrero covering most of his face, he followed Raul to the doorway and peered out.

''This way,'' Raul whispered, motioning Slocum down

a narrow road lined with small adobe houses.

They left quietly, walking on the balls of their feet while keeping to the darkest shadows.

Jose was short, scarcely five feet tall. He stood beside a rear door into the two-story building where Slocum had been taken when he first came to Guerrero. As Raul led Slocum down a dark alley to the back of the cantina, Jose beckoned to them. He held a finger to his lips and whispered, "*Silencio.*"

Slocum saw Jose's serape and had an idea. "Give me this, so I will look like the others," he whispered.

Jose nodded and slipped the serape over his head.

Slocum took off the sombrero and put Jose's serape over his shoulders. With the sombrero on his head, his shadow looked like those of the natives in Guerrero. He'd been shown to a small stable where his grullo gelding and Chico's pinto were saddled and tied. He knew the route he would take when he made his run to reach the horses.

He drew his Bowie knife from his boot and concealed it under the serape, after checking the loads in the .44 Raul had given him. A moment passed. He took a deep breath and carefully open the door without saying a word, his senses keen, his heart racing. Jose and Raul slipped away quietly into the dark as Slocum crept into the building.

The cantina was empty. Moving as softly as his size would allow, he tiptoed over to a set of stairs leading to the second floor. Being careful not to make a noise, he moved up each of the steps one by one after first testing for a sound that might give him away to anyone upstairs.

He crept to the top to a darkened hallway, where he waited for his eyes to adjust to poor light. A window at the end of the hall admitted a pale glow from stars in a clear night sky. There, in front of a door, Slocum saw an outline, a figure slumped in a chair against one wall.

Moving as softly as he could, he inched down the hall with his knife hidden beneath Jose's serape. As he got closer to the figure, he saw more detail. Juanito was asleep, his head lolled to one side, his sombrero resting on the floor beside him. But as Slocum came closer, suddenly a floorboard creaked underneath his boot.

Juanito jerked, turning his head in Slocum's direction. For a few precious seconds he did not move while Slocum came toward him.

"Quien es?" Juanito asked, still seated in his chair, not expecting trouble.

"Diego," Slocum answered softly, walking faster, only a few yards from Juanito now.

"Quien?" Juanito asked again, hearing an unfamiliar voice.

Slocum reached the chair just as Juanito sprang suddenly to his feet. Sweeping the serape aside, Slocum grinned savagely. "I am Diego," he snarled. "John is my name in English."

Juanito clawed for one pistol. Slocum sent the blade of his bowie into the Mexican's breastbone with the force of a sledgehammer blow. Cartilage snapped like dry kindling when the tip of the knife pierced Juanito's ribs, while at the same time Slocum made a grab for the Mexican's gun with his free hand, keeping it from leaving its holster. As he drove his blade all the way into its hilt, he lifted the brim of Pedro's sombrero so Juanito got a good look at his face in the starlight coming from a window at the end of the hallway.

Air rushed from Juanito's lungs—he was driven back against the wall, pinioned there, his eyes bulging with pain and fear as Slocum's knife entered his heart.

"Die quietly, you rotten son of a bitch!" Slocum hissed, his face only inches from Juanito's.

"How . . . ?" Juanito gasped.

Slocum twisted his knife, doing as much damage as he could, hearing bone and gristle pop inside the Mexican's chest when the heavy blade turned between broken ribs. Blood showered over his hand and the knife handle, dribbling to the floor like rain from a leaking roof.

He jerked the knife free, letting Juanito's body slide down the wall to the floor with a thump. Slocum took both pistols from Juanito's gunbelt and stuck them in the waistband of his denims. Air bubbled from the dying Mexican's mouth while Slocum tried to open the door. He found the door locked, and threw his shoulder against it, splintering the door frame on his first try to enter the room.

He saw a woman bolt upright on a bed across the room. To calm her fears he said softly, "Don't worry, Alice. I'm from Texas—your sister sent me. Get dressed and we're getting out of here as quick as we can."

The woman, wearing a nightgown, didn't move. She wore a surprised expression on her face.

"Get dressed!" he commanded. "We're running out of time!"

As though she suddenly realized what was happening, the girl leapt from her bed to don a pair of pants draped over a chair in one corner of the bedroom.

Slocum hurried over to her. "No time for anything else," he said. "My name is John Slocum, and tonight you and I are in for the ride of our lives. Follow me." He took her by the arm and led her into the hallway.

When Alice saw the body and smelled blood pooled near the door she drew in a quick breath, but before she had time to utter a word, Slocum was pulling her toward the stairs.

They hurried down the steps two at a time and turned for the back door. Sheathing his bloody bowie knife, Slocum drew one of his pistols before he pulled Alice into the alley.

"Run," he said, taking her by the arm. "We've got a couple of horses waiting for us. I sure as hell hope you can ride."

"I can ride as well as any man," Alice replied, and by the tone of her voice, he knew she meant it, although her words were slurred by laudanum.

They ran east down a darkened alleyway, toward the little stable where the grulla and the pinto were tied. The girl was barefoot, and at times she stumbled over something unseen in the inky blackness. Covering their progress with a pistol, Slocum ran as fast as Alice could travel, his heart pounding. If they could make it through the gates out of Guerrero without being discovered, they stood a fighting chance of making it back to the border alive.

They were both gasping for air by the time they reached the stable. Jose was there to swing open a gate, and stood back as they mounted horses. Slocum swung aboard the grulla after helping the girl into the saddle, giving Alice the pinto. Wheeling his gelding, Slocum led the way out of the barn, turning south.

They galloped down empty streets, awakening the village dogs with pounding hooves. Alice swayed dangerously in the saddle, yet she held on to the saddlehorn with a look of grim determination on her face.

Racing toward the gate out of Guerrero, Slocum saw a sleeping Mexican near the opening toss his blanket aside to sit up in his bedroll, staring at the pair of galloping horses. Slocum and Alice raced through the gap in the stone wall at full speed, leaning over their horses' necks.

Not a shot was fired when they rode away from the village. But Slocum knew their run for freedom had only just begun. He looked over his shoulder. Lanterns all over Guerrero were springing to life, and he could hear angry shouts above the rattle of their racing iron horseshoes. The dogs had awakened people in the village, and it would not be long before Luis Zambrano came after them.

22

Where the land was hilly, Slocum stayed off the skyline to keep from being too easily seen by Zambrano and anyone who might be with him following their tracks. Slocum hoped for a chance to slow them down across sunbaked ground, where their hoofprints would be harder to find. Down in his gut he knew Zambrano was as certain of their direction as *he* was—north, to the Texas border, and safety for himself and the girl.

He glanced up at the rising sun. Four or five hours of hard riding remained to reach Sabinas. By tonight, if they made it to nightfall, pursuit would come more slowly. Whoever was reading their tracks would have to be skillful, of necessity, taking more time getting it done. Slocum knew he was faced with a very dangerous gamble after sunset; ride open country where travel was slower but they would be harder to find, or strike the main road north of Sabinas that led to Laredo, where there were no obstacles, nothing to slow a horse down, merely mile after mile of roadway through the desert. It would be far more dangerous to ride through the brush, giving Zambrano time to send someone ahead along the main road to cut them off. But sticking to the brushlands offered less risk of an all-out gun battle.

First, Zambrano would have to find them before any shooting started. The desert offered countless places to hide, but no water for themselves or their horses. A choice had to be made when the sun went down, and a bad guess could cost them their lives.

Trotting their mounts, galloping now and then, they pushed steadily northeast to circle Sabinas and hit the Laredo road. And always, on the horizon behind them, he watched for a cloud of dust.

At mid-morning, Slocum saw what he expected to see, the dust and faint outlines of two riders. "I don't see how they can be gaining on us," Slocum said, when they crossed a brushy knob with a better view to the southwest. "It don't make any sense. . . ."

Alice, her head finally clear of the effects of laudanum, watched the dust and tiny specks beneath it. Her complexion had turned white, making bruises more evident on her cheeks. She shaded her eyes from the sun with a small hand. "It almost looks like some of those horses don't have riders," she said, "only I can't be sure at this distance."

Slocum stood in his stirrups, squinting into the heat haze to see the dark spots below the caliche cloud. "I think that's the answer," he said, trying to keep the pronouncement from sounding too grim. "They brought spare horses. They must be changing mounts every few miles. Smart. Whoever formed that plan knows how to cross a desert in a hurry."

"They're going to catch up to us, aren't they?" she asked, as if she already knew the answer.

Slocum hurried his grulla off the knob, down a winding ravine so shallow it was barely noticeable as a dry wash until they rode directly into it. "If they do, little lady, they'll get a taste of lead. It'll be soon enough. Then some of the advantages take a turn our way. If I can find the right place to make a stand, I can pick 'em off. It'll slow them down when I start to shoot. They won't be coming so all-fired fast when I toss a few bullets their way.''

Alice was looking at the pistols he'd taken from Juanito, which were stuck in the waistband of his pants. ''I can shoot,'' she said. ''Dad taught me how to shoot when I was real young, before he died. If you'll give me one of those guns, maybe I can help if they get in pistol range.''

He admired her spunk, and told her so. ''You're tougher than I imagined you'd be, Alice Drake. If you say you can shoot, I believe you.'' He handed her one of the .44's. ''Don't waste any shells. We aren't exactly overloaded with ammunition.''

Looping her reins around her saddlehorn, she opened the .44's loading gate and inspected the brass cartridge caps by rolling the cylinder with her thumb. Without saying a word, she tucked the revolver into the top of her pants and hid it beneath her nightgown.

Riding the ravine at a gallop, they continued north as fast as weary horses could travel.

Behind a rocky outcrop, hidden by darkness and a crown of yucca plants growing around the top of the ledge, Slocum raised his Winchester to his shoulder, being careful to keep the barrel from reflecting starlight by holding it in a shadow cast by a fan of spiked yucca leaves. Two riders came down a creek bed single file, following its dry bottom. One leaned down from his saddle reading their hoofprints in the sand. This was the man Slocum planned to execute, the expert tracker who guided Luis Zambrano so unerringly no matter how hard Slocum tried to throw off pursuit by crossing hard ground. The tracker wore no hat and had shoulder-length hair, probably a Yaqui Indian judging by his appearance from a distance, perhaps one of the Guerrero residents Zambrano trusted when it came to reading sign in the desert.

Alice waited behind the outcrop holding their horses, with instructions to keep them from nickering at all costs. Surprise was the key element Slocum needed to slow down Zambrano and his tracker in the dark. When they found out he'd stopped running and was ready to fight, they would be more cautious. He figured he could drop the front rider with his first shot, if he got the right range. Then Zambrano would hurry to find cover, and by then he and Alice would be moving north again.

Waiting, sighting in on the tracker's chest, he silenced the voice of his conscience for what he was about to do. Shooting an unsuspecting man for any reason, ambushing him without warning, was something he'd only done in wartime. But in many respects this was a war, and he closed his mind to what he was about to do. Killing or wounding this man was necessary in order to have a chance to get the girl back to Texas.

The scout halted his horse in the sandy bottom of the draw to gaze down at their hoofprints. This was Slocum's chance, when he knew he could not miss.

He gently nudged the rifle's trigger. A thundering report ended the desert silence. The Winchester slammed into his shoulder, yellow flame spitting from its barrel as the explosion echoed across the brushlands surrounding the dry stream. The tracker jerked in his saddle, emitting a piercing scream when he was torn from the back of his plunging, rearing horse. The Yaqui fell, clutching his shoulder, rocking back and forth in pain as his cry became a softer moan.

Slocum levered another shell, swinging his gun sights to Zambrano. With fractions of a second to get his aim he squeezed off a second shot, wincing when the roar of his gun came so close to his right ear. But the big Mexican had surprisingly been too quick for him and wheeled his horse into a mesquite thicket just ahead of the bullet.

Quickly ejecting the spent cartridge, Slocum readied a third shell.

Slocum almost took another shot at a shadow before he lowered his rifle—he couldn't be sure of a hit, and ammunition for his Winchester was too precious to waste. He crawled backward and stood up, trotting down the back side of the outcrop with the scent of burnt gunpowder filling his nose.

"Let's get out of here," he told Alice, swinging aboard the grulla.

They were off at a steady lope through an opening in tight tangles of thorny brush, riding northeast to strike the road to Laredo. Slocum had made a decision earlier that night—to make this a horse race, after he gave Zambrano's scout a little taste of hot lead. Too much time had been wasted winding through cactus and mesquite. The moment had come to ask their horses for all they had.

Alice rode up alongside him where a wide spot in the brush gave her room. "How many did you shoot?" she asked in a voice he barely heard above the rattle of shod hooves. "You fired two times."

"I dropped one of them," he answered quietly, not wanting to think about the way he'd done it from ambush. "I got the man who was reading our tracks. Maybe it'll slow Zambrano down a bit now that he lost his tracker."

She cast a quick look over her shoulder. Although she did not say anything about his marksmanship, her silence was enough to convince him that she was worried over the fact that Zambrano was still alive.

He thought about the man he'd wounded. Shooting him from ambush wasn't his style, but under the circumstances he'd had no real choice.

The road was empty, pale caliche ruts stretching across mile after mile of desert illuminated by stars and a piece of

moon. A coyote barked off in the distance. Night birds
whistled to each other from mesquite limbs on either side
of the ruts. For several hours they had the road to themselves. Slocum pushed the grulla now, forcing Alice's pinto
to keep up. The little horse was game, but too short-coupled
to carry her without tiring easily at much of a pace. Tom's
big grulla handled Slocum's weight without effort. The
horses were gaunt-flanked from lack of water after so many
punishing miles through desert heat. Slocum's lips were
dry, cracking, and he knew the girl was suffering too. But
to her credit, she made no complaint whatsoever, riding
beside him at a fast trot as casually as if they were in no
danger at all.

"Whatever my sister's paying you to do this, it won't
be enough to make up for what you've done," she said
after several minutes of silence. "You've got a lot of guts,
John Slocum, more than any man I ever met. You haven't
told me much about yourself, only that you're a detective
for the railroads sometimes and that you deal in good-
blooded horses up in Denver."

"There ain't all that much to tell really. I'm on the move
quite a bit. Never was inclined to stay in one place very
long."

"I suppose that means you don't have a wife."

"No wife. Never found a woman who could tolerate me
for all that long, I reckon."

"No regular girlfriends?"

"Not so you'd notice. I've got a few lady friends I see
from time to time, but nothing you'd call regular."

After a moment, Alice asked, "Have you ever wanted to
stay with a woman you loved?"

He glanced up at the sky, thinking about an honest answer to her question. "It's fair to say I've loved a good
share of women in my time, but I get this urge to wander
pretty often. I get an itch to see what's on the other side of

the mountain, so to speak. Some men aren't built to stay in the same place. I reckon I'm part of that breed."

"Young men my age are too childish," she said. "They act silly as a goose when a woman looks them in the eye. I can't stand foolish-acting men. My sister says I'm too particular when it comes to men. I suppose that's why I thought I was in love with Carl Smith. This whole thing is my fault, because I let him show me how good laudanum makes you feel sometimes."

He didn't offer an opinion on that subject. She was blaming herself enough as it was. Alice was a girl older than her years, it seemed, but right now he faced more pressing matters than a girl's tastes in men. Getting out of this part of Mexico alive promised to be more of a chore than he'd first figured.

Later, off in the distance, he spied a small adobe hut west of the road. A few taller mesquites grew in clusters near the house. "There'll be water at that adobe," he said, thinking out loud. "Maybe whoever lives there won't mind giving us some for our horses."

"I hope so. This paint horse is coughing from the dust all the time now."

"Some folks down here don't like Americans all that much. I hope these are friendly. It's late, close to midnight. We could get shot at, so stay back while I ask at the house if we can water these animals."

They rode to a narrow lane running to the house. As soon as they turned down the lane, a dog began to bark near the adobe. A moment later a lantern flickered to life behind one of the windows. Slocum kept his right hand near the butt of Raul's gun as they approached the front of the hut.

They stopped twenty yards from the house. A bare-chested man holding a lantern peered around his door frame. The dog stopped barking.

Slocum edged his horse closer. "Señor, may we have a

few buckets of water for our horses? We are travelers and I have a woman with me. We mean you no harm.''

For several seconds the man said nothing. Then he pointed to a well beside his house. *"Como no, Señor,"* he replied.

"We can have water," Slocum told Alice over his shoulder, swinging down from the saddle. Then he spoke to the Mexican. *"Muchas gracias, Señor."* It was about as much Spanish as he could manage.

Slocum went to the well, finding a bucket on a piece of rope. He sent the bucket down, casting a wary look back along the road by which they had come, finding it empty.

Maybe we'll make it after all, he thought, giving water to each of their horses. Shooting the scout appeared to have given them a considerable lead again.

Looking north, he knew they weren't far from Aguas Calientes. They faced another brutal stretch of desert to the border, miles of dry road and killing heat that would take a terrible toll on their horses after daybreak. Remembering the distance, Slocum decided it was too soon to think they could make it ahead of an experienced Mexican bandit like Zambrano who knew this country.

After drinking himself and giving Alice all the water she wanted, he tightened their saddle cinches. He wanted their mounts to be as ready as possible for a horse race.

They rode away from the little hut, after Slocum thanked the owner again for giving them water. Back on the main road to Laredo, they turned north. Beneath a velvety night sky they struck a steady trot, having the road to themselves.

Much later, when his eyelids had grown heavy, they passed through Aguas Calientes while the village was asleep. Slocum was briefly reminded of Pedro Gonzalez and the goat meat they'd shared there. He forced his thoughts to other matters, thinking how peaceful things had seemed since he'd fired those shots from the rocks. Was it possible that shooting Zambrano's Indian tracker had been enough to turn the bandit back?

A little voice inside his head told him how foolish this notion was. More of a feeling than anything else, he sensed trouble was close at their heels, getting closer with each passing hour.

23

Dawn came clear and still to the Tamaulipas desert south of Laredo. Alice's pinto had begun to limp, and when Slocum got down to examine its right forefoot, he found a stone bruise in the frog of the hoof.

Surrounded by gently rolling desert hills thick with cactus and mesquite and yucca, Slocum guessed they were only ten or fifteen miles from Nuevo Laredo, the Rio Grande River, and safety from Zambrano.

"Let's keep movin'," he told Alice, climbing back aboard the grullo. "It's not far now."

"I feel sorry for this horse," she said, her face pink from sun and a difficult, exhausting ride.

"The pinto'll have plenty of time to heal up once we cross that river."

They moved out at a jog trot. The pinto's lameness would only grow worse, yet Slocum found himself hoping the spotted horse could hold out for another dozen miles or so.

Morning shadows brightened, shortening beneath saguaro cactus and mesquite trunks as the sun came above the horizon. Slocum's neck was sore from looking backward to see if Zambrano was behind them.

This early, they still had the road to themselves, and had seen only a few travelers coming from the north during the night hours.

"We're going to make it," Alice said, her thin voice filled with hope. "I just know we are."

Slocum was almost, but not quite, willing to agree. Ten or fifteen miles could turn out to be dangerous ground to cover if Zambrano had somehow ridden around them, using his spare horse to cover more territory across the brushlands.

No sense in worrying about it, he told himself, checking his guns for full loads. Whatever happens, I aim to be ready for it as I can be.

It was as they crested a gently sloping rise in the road that he saw a sight that made him jerk his grulla to a halt. A huge Mexican in a drooping sombrero was waiting for them in the middle of the road, sitting casually on a lathered buckskin horse with a spare chestnut gelding tied to his saddlehorn.

"It's him!" Alice gasped.

"I'm afraid so, Miss Drake," Slocum told her. "Turn that horse around and ride back until you're out of sight. I'll ride out to meet him and we'll settle this. We can't outrun him with your horse being lame, so it's gonna come down to a gunfight and I don't want you in the way where a stray bullet might hit you."

"Be careful, John," she said, turning the limping pinto to ride back down the ruts.

Slocum jerked his Winchester free and chambered a cartridge before he started toward Zambrano. The bearded giant was a quarter of a mile away with a rifle resting across the pommel of his saddle.

This is it, Slocum thought. We're about to find out who's got the best aim from the greatest distance.

He kept the grulla moving forward at a walk, ready to swing his rifle up the moment Zambrano moved. On either side of the Mexican bandit, thicker stands of scrub mesquite trees would give him cover if he fired and then swung off the Laredo road, leaving Slocum out in the open to dodge lead.

When they were roughly three hundred yards apart, Zambrano yelled at him, and his voice carried sharp and clear in the early morning stillness.

"Hey, *gringo bastardo*! You have my woman, and you no give me the gold promised in the telegram!"

"I never intended to pay you a goddamn cent, you yellow son of a bitch!" Slocum bellowed back, his temper on the rise. "I meant to kill you, only I wanted to be sure the girl was safe in Texas before I blow a hole through you the size of a tortilla!"

"You talk very tough, *bastardo*!" Zambrano cried. "Let us see if you are as good with a gun and as tough as you say you are!"

Suddenly, Zambrano swung his rifle up and triggered off a quick shot. The slug flew through the crown of Slocum's Stetson as he fired back his .44-caliber answer. Slocum's hat fell to the caliche road behind him, and he felt the sting of a flesh wound across the top of his scalp while the Winchester shot forth a finger of flame and a ball of molten lead.

But Zambrano's horse was already moving, and Slocum's shot was a miss, inches to the left. Working the loading lever as fast as he could, he saw he was too slow when Zambrano steadied his rifle muzzle to fire again.

An unexpected explosion came from the mesquite trees to Zambrano's right, the mighty roar of a shotgun. Zambrano's horse shied as his white cotton shirt and sombrero brim were shredded by shotgun pellets.

Then blood squirted from dozens of wounds in the Mexican's face, neck, and side. He let out a groan as his plunging horse fought the pull on its reins, trying to escape the noise and a few stray shotgun pellets striking its golden hide. The chestnut broke free and trotted off into the brush.

Slocum took careful aim, wondering who had fired the shotgun at Zambrano from such close range. Zambrano had an enemy he had not counted on.

Slocum pulled the trigger, his rifle spitting fire and hot lead amid the clap of an explosion near his ear.

Zambrano was jerked backward out of his saddle with tremendous force, as though he'd run into an invisible wire strung across the road. He went off the rump of his dun, landing on the back of his neck and his shoulders, his sombrero floating lazily above him until it fluttered to the ground, its cone-shaped crown full of pellet holes.

"Who the hell?" Slocum asked aloud, jacking another shell into his rifle, wondering who was hiding in the mesquites, who would have the nerve to shoot Luis Zambrano at very close range.

He waited, covering the trees, until a Mexican in a straw sombrero rode out of the brush on the sorrel gelding Slocum had borrowed from Marshal Tom Spence.

"I'll be damned," Slocum said with a sigh, recognizing the young Mexican at once. He lowered his rifle and kicked the grulla to a short lope to ride up to Raul.

"How did you get here ahead of us?" Slocum asked when he saw Raul looking down at Zambrano's bloodied face.

"I know some of the old *bandido* trails. I rode this good horse Pedro rode when he came to Guerrero, and it is a very good runner with lots of wind."

"But why did you come here? I thought I agreed to meet you and Jose across the river in Laredo."

Raul's thin face turned to granite. He continued to stare down at Zambrano. The bandit was still breathing, moaning, his wounds leaking blood into a worn wagon rut in the caliche. "I come to kill him, Señor Slocum, because he forced me to shoot my own cousin. I knew he would kill me if I refused. It is a very small thing to the family of Pedro Gonzalez, but now I have my revenge."

Slocum gave him a weak grin as Alice Drake came riding up to them. "You've got a lot of guts, Raul. So does your friend Jose, and I intend to see that you're both rewarded well. We'd have never gotten out of Guerrero without your help."

Tears filled Raul's eyes. "What I have done will not bring Pedro back. I believed I owed it to Pedro to do this thing, even if it cost me my life."

Slocum noticed Zambrano's eyes were open, eyelids fluttering as he moaned and groaned. He swung down and walked over to the fallen bandit.

"How does it feel, asshole, to know you're dyin'?" Slocum asked.

Zambrano's black eyes filled with hatred. "I should have killed you the day you came to Guerrero, *bastardo*," he said as blood oozed from his twisted lips.

"You got greedy, you dumb son of bitch. You wanted that gold, more than this girl's sister was willing to pay. And now you're gonna pay for bein' greedy by bleedin' to death right here in this wagon road. We're gonna sit right here an' watch you die. And in case it matters, it was Raul, Pedro's cousin, who blasted all them holes in you with a shotgun. He was settlin' a score for what you ordered him to do to Pedro. Think about it, you ugly son of a bitch, while you're lyin' there dyin', slowly bleedin' to death. Raul got even with you, and he'll still be alive to piss on your grave."

A series of tremors began to shake the big bandit's legs and arms. His eyes wouldn't stay open.

"Feel those shakes?" Slocum asked. "They call 'em

death throes. Means you're dyin', only I hope like hell it takes you quite a spell so we can watch. I'm enjoyin' the hell out of this an' so is Raul. I 'spect the little lady here is likin' it too, after the beatings you gave her. So lie there an' shake until you die, you yellow bastard. Maybe this hot sun will cause your eyeballs to boil and burst before you pass on. I've heard tell it hurts like hell when a man's eyeballs pop in a real hot sun.''

Zambrano coughed, and then his right boot began to twitch so violently it rattled the rowel on his spur. Blood came faster from his lips now.

Raul got off the sorrel and stood over Zambrano with his feet spread apart. ''This is for Pedro Gonzalez,'' he snarled as he puckered his lips and then spat upon Luis Zambrano's face.

''It's finally over,'' Alice whispered, her face the color of snow.

Slocum nodded. ''You'll be back in Abilene with your sister on the first train we can catch out of Laredo.'' He looked over to Raul. ''What will you do, my friend? After you come with us to Laredo so I can draw some reward money out of the bank?''

''I will collect the one-thousand-peso reward being offered for Luis Zambrano by the *federales* in Nuevo Laredo, Señor. It is not much money, but I will give it to Pedro's family. It is all I can do for them now.''

''You didn't have a choice,'' Slocum assured him.

Zambrano let out a whispering breath, and then his chest went still.

''He's dead,'' Slocum said. He spoke to Raul again. ''Go out yonder an' fetch his horse an' I'll help you tie his body across his saddle. The three of us will ride together to Nuevo Laredo, an' then after you collect the reward for Zambrano here in Mexico, we'll meet at Marshal Tom Spence's office so I can give you some of the gold this woman's sister was offering for her return. As far as I'm concerned, you've earned a big share of it.''

"*Gracias, Señor,*" Raul said. "I will go and find the horses and I will take this dead bandido to the *federale comandante* in Nuevo Laredo.''

Tom Spence embraced him when Slocum walked in his office with Alice Drake. "Boy, am I ever glad to see you.'' He stared past Slocum at the girl. "Looks like you already got what you came for without havin' to carry that money across the river.''

"I had some help,'' Slocum answered. "And I appreciate the offer of help you sent in that telegram. I knew who that banker from Laredo was gonna be.''

Tom grinned. "I always did take a fancy to workin' in a place where there was plenty of money, carryin' plenty of it around with me, even if it wasn't mine. Now you've gone an' robbed me of my first bankin' job.''

Slocum chuckled, then said, "I need to send a wire off to Amanda in Abilene, to tell her I've got her sister back an' that she's okay. There'll be a young Mexican by the name of Raul who is comin' over to collect part of the reward money. I'll have to go to the bank and draw some of it out. It's a long story, how we got here. I'll tell it to you over some good whiskey, soon as I get Miss Alice Drake a room at the best hotel. She'll be wantin' a hot bathtub an' some decent food.''

Alice smiled. "I may just join the two of you later,'' she told Marshal Spence. "That is, if you gentlemen don't mind.''

"Never turned down the company of a pretty lady,'' Tom said as they made for the office door.

As they walked out on Laredo's dusty main street, Alice

took Slocum by the arm. "Be sure you tell Amanda that I'm fine, and I expect to see her soon."

A sly grin lifted one corner of Slocum's mouth. "I expect to see her real soon myself," he said, hoping he would spend a wonderful night in Amanda's upstairs bedroom.

24

Amanda Drake watched him over the rim of a crystal goblet full of brandy while he told her the story of Alice's rescue. A lantern burned low on her dressing table. A soft night wind fluttered the lace curtains framing her bedroom windows. Alice was back at the family home on the west edge of Abilene where they had lived before their parents died. Earlier, as she and Slocum got off the train, the sisters had had a tearful reunion.

"She's learned her lesson, I think," Slocum said, tasting his third glass of brandy. "She won't ever be inclined to try laudanum again, an' I think she'll be a little more careful about choosing a man's company."

"She fell hard for Carl Smith," Amanda remembered. "I tried to tell her he was a no-good gambler, but she wouldn't listen. I had no idea he was working for this cruel Mexican bandit, going from town to town looking for a white women to become his love slave."

"There's no trace of this Carl Smith," Slocum told her. "I doubt if it's his real name anyway. Marshal Spence and I covered Laredo asking questions about him. Nobody'd seen him since he crossed over into Nuevo Laredo with the girl to collect his money from Zambrano."

"The two young Mexicans . . . you said their names were Raul and Jose. Without them, Alice might still be a prisoner of Zambrano and you might be dead."

"Can't deny that, Amanda. I gave 'em each five hundred in gold. I brought the rest of your reward money back."

She smiled. "I still owe you five thousand dollars," she said.

"I hardly feel like I earned the money," he replied.

"You did. You killed that terrible Mexican who held my sister, and you got her back to me safely. I'd say you earned every cent."

He shrugged. "The girl has a few bruises from times Zambrano slapped her around, but a doctor in Laredo said she was okay to travel by train." He looked down at his glass. "There's still a chance for bad news," he continued. "She could be carrying a baby by Zambrano. Won't know until a few more weeks pass."

"I pray she isn't," Amanda said softly, "but I'd rather have her back pregnant than knowing she was a prisoner of that evil man for the rest of her life."

"He won't be botherin' anybody else," Slocum assured her. "Raul and I made sure of that."

She got up off the bed to pour herself and Slocum more brandy. "Not only did you rid Texas and Mexico of the bandit and his gang, you shot that bully Justin Davis and one of his gunmen. This whole town will be grateful when I give them the news. Davis was a terror in the saloon district. Marshal Bill Hatcher was scared to death of him and wouldn't intervene when we needed him. You've solved two big problems for me, and the citizens of Abilene have benefitted too."

"I didn't plan it. Davis and three more tried to ambush me in Mexico. I'm sure they were headed for Guerrero to try to get the reward you'd offered for your sister."

"It would have made me sick to my stomach if I'd had

to pay Davis for Alice's return. But I would have done it. I would have done anything to get her back, including making a deal with the Devil himself.''

''Is that who you think I am?'' he asked, grinning a little. ''Do I look like ol' Satan? I hadn't noticed my horns, although I do have a scratch on top of my head where Zambrano's first shot almost got me. Ruined a perfectly good Stetson hat instead.''

Amanda smiled impishly. ''You do have a devilish side, Mr. John Slocum. I can tell by the way your eyes roam to the front of my dressing gown.''

''Can't help myself, pretty lady. When I see something I really like, I can't keep my eyes off it no matter how hard I try.''

She walked over to the bed and downed the entire contents of her goblet in a single gulp. ''Would you care to see a little more of me, John?'' she asked, and now her voice sounded husky. She wasn't smiling when she said it.

''It's a silly question,'' he answered, tossing back the rest of his drink. ''A man who wouldn't want to see more of you would have to be plumb loco.''

She reached for the sash binding her gown, opening it. Then she let it slide off her shoulders and fall to the bedroom floor. ''Do you still like what you see?'' she wanted to know, staring at his face with luminous eyes.

''It's even better than I'd imagined, Amanda,'' he said as he stood up to unbutton his shirt. ''You're one hell of a woman, in more ways than one.''

He walked over to her and took her in his arms. She gazed up at him.

''I don't take strangers to my bed,'' she said, a mock look of seriousness pinching her brow.

He bent down and kissed her full lips, then cupped one generous breast in a palm. ''Let me introduce myself,'' he said in a hoarse, lust-filled tone. "My name is John Slocum, and we aren't strangers any longer."

Amanda moaned and pulled him gently down on the bed. He kissed her again, more hungrily this time.

"Take me, John," she whispered, the sweet smell of brandy on her breath. "It's been such a very long time since I've been with a man."

He rolled to one side of the bed, pulled off his boots, and then shucked his denims, dropping them on the floor.

"Please turn down the lamp a little," Amanda purred. "And perhaps you should close the windows."

"Why's that?" he asked, twisting the lamp wick down to a pinpoint of soft light. He got up and walked over to the windows before she answered him.

She was smiling when she said, "I make a lot of noise when a real man's making love to me, and I can see by the size of your cock that I won't be able to control myself tonight. I wouldn't want everyone on this side of Abilene to know how much I'm enjoying myself."

He chuckled as he pulled the windows down. His swelling cock was greeted by a dainty hand when he returned to the bed, and seconds later, a pair of warm, wet lips encircled his member while a tongue went to work on his glans.

This is gonna be the best part of the reward, he thought, pushing everything else from his mind.